The Music Festival Mystery

At the back of the entrance hall, a wide stairway led to the upper floors of the dormitory. Bess and George were staying with Penny and Joann on the first floor, while Nancy was staying with Dina on the second floor.

After leaving the girls, Nancy and Dina went upstairs to her room. At the top of the stairs Dina turned left, along a narrow corridor. Each room door had a whiteboard attached to it, with the names of the occupants at the top and a marker dangling from a string. Nancy noted some of the messages on the boards as she walked past.

"Lynn—meet at library." "Hi, Kevin, catch you later, Pat." "HELP—e-mail me calc assignment ASAP, Josie."

Dina came to a sudden stop next to one of the doors. The stiff way she held her shoulders alerted Nancy. Something was wrong. Nancy walked faster, then broke into a run.

Dina was staring at her whiteboard. Below her name was a crude drawing of a heart with a dagger sticking through it.

Nancy Drew
Mystery Stories

Available from MINSTREL Books

NANCY DREW® 157

THE
MUSIC FESTIVAL MYSTERY

CAROLYN KEENE

A MINSTREL® BOOK

Published by POCKET BOOKS
New York   London   Toronto   Sydney   Singapore

This book is a work of fiction. Names, characters, places and incidents are products of the author's imagination or are used fictitiously. Any resemblance to actual events or locales or persons living or dead is entirely coincidental.

A MINSTREL PAPERBACK *Original*

A Minstrel Book published by
POCKET BOOKS, a division of Simon & Schuster, Inc.
1230 Avenue of the Americas, New York, NY 10020

Copyright © 2000 by Simon & Schuster, Inc.

ISBN: 0-671-04265-3

First Minstrel Books printing November 2000

10 9 8 7 6 5 4 3 2 1

NANCY DREW, NANCY DREW MYSTERY STORIES, A MINSTREL BOOK and colophon are registered trademarks of Simon & Schuster, Inc.

Cover art by Franco Accornero

Printed in the U.S.A.

Contents

THE
MUSIC FESTIVAL MYSTERY

1

Festival Weekend

Nancy Drew spotted the green-and-white sign she'd been looking for: Exit 9A—Emerson College. She put on her blinker and steered her blue Mustang convertible off the interstate onto the exit ramp. As she neared the intersection, the light changed to red. She braked to a halt and tucked a strand of reddish blond hair behind one ear.

"We're almost there," she announced.

From the backseat, Nancy's friend Bess Marvin said, "Good thing. I'm starved!"

Bess's cousin George Fayne was in the front passenger seat. She laughed at Bess's announcement. "Duh," she said. "Admit it, Bess—you're always starved!"

Nancy glanced over her shoulder. The warm breeze

had tousled Bess's long blond hair and put a gleam in her bright blue eyes.

Bess folded her arms across her chest and gave a little shiver.

"Are you chilly?" Nancy asked with concern. "Should we put the top up?"

"Chilly? No way!" Bess replied. "I'm excited, that's all. I *love* world music, but I practically never get to hear any of it live. Why don't we have a festival like this back in River Heights?"

"Nobody to organize one, I guess," George said. She pulled her red-and-blue cap a little lower over her dark brown curls.

The light changed. Nancy turned right onto Campus Road.

George leaned forward to switch radio stations. A burst of syncopated drumbeats sounded over a thumping bass, and then a high voice wailed in a language Nancy didn't recognize. After a few moments the music faded.

"It's Friday and you're tuned to ECR, Emerson College Radio," the announcer said. "And that was the Rai Rebels, from Algeria."

"Wow!" Bess exclaimed. She grabbed George's shoulder. "I've got their CD. They are awesome!"

"The Rai Rebels are just one of the big attractions at this weekend's Worldbeat Festival," the announcer continued. "We'll tape all the performances for future

2

broadcast. But if you want to hear them and all the other fantastic bands live, better get your tickets today. They're going fast!"

"Uh-oh—I hope we can get in," George said.

"Don't worry," Nancy replied. A tune with a strong Latin beat came on. "Ned took care of getting tickets. He lined up places for us to stay, too."

Ned Nickerson was Nancy's longtime boyfriend. He was a student at Emerson College.

"I didn't know Ned was such a fan of world music," George remarked.

"He's not especially," Nancy told her. "But the president of the club that's sponsoring the festival is a friend of his—a guy named Cyril. He's from Australia."

"An Aussie?" Bess said. "Cool. Is he cute? Does he have an accent?"

"Does he have a pet kangaroo?" George joked.

Nancy grinned. "No idea. You'll have to find out for yourselves. Anyway, it's really important to him for the festival to be a big success. So naturally Ned's pitching in. And, I don't know . . . I got a feeling there may be something funny going on. The kind of thing we might be able to help with."

"A mystery, you mean?" George asked quickly.

Nancy had a big reputation as a detective, and both George and Bess often helped in her investigations.

"Nothing I can put my finger on," Nancy said.

"But it wouldn't hurt to keep an eye out for any problems."

"That's exciting," Bess said eagerly. "What about the Rai Rebels? Will they be around all weekend? Do you think I could meet them?"

Nancy and George laughed.

"Where are we meeting Ned?" George asked.

"He said to call him when we got there," Nancy replied. "Would you do it?"

George's shoulder bag was on the floor in front of her seat. She rummaged around and pulled out her cell phone. "What's the number?" she asked.

After Nancy told her, she punched in the numbers. In a second she said, "Hi, Ned, it's me, George. We're here, on Campus Road. Um, let me look. . . . We just passed Harding Lane. Okay, see you."

She disconnected and turned to Nancy. "He says to park by the gym. He'll meet us there."

Nancy turned through a stone arch onto the Emerson campus. The lawns on either side of the tree-lined road were thick with students talking, reading, and playing Frisbee in the spring sunshine. Nancy followed the signs to the gym parking lot and pulled into a vacant space.

"Emerson College," she said, reaching for the button that raised the top. "Last stop."

Nancy got out of the car and straightened up. As she glanced around, she felt her heart give an extra thump.

Ned was striding across the parking lot toward them. A huge grin lit up his handsome face and dark eyes.

"Hey, there," he called. A moment later he was giving Nancy a hug that lifted her off her feet. As he put her down, he whispered in her ear, "I've missed you so much."

"I've missed you, too," Nancy whispered back.

After Ned said hi to Bess and George, the three girls retrieved their backpacks from the trunk. Then the group set off across campus.

"I told Cyril and some of the others we'd meet them at the student center," Ned said. "Are you hungry? We can get a bite while we're there."

"Sounds good," Nancy replied. Bess gave her a grateful look. "What's the program?"

"After you meet some of the gang, we'll get you settled in," Ned said. "I've got a festival steering committee meeting at six. You wouldn't believe how many last-minute details we have to take care of."

"What should we do about dinner?" Nancy asked.

"No problem," Ned assured her. "If you can wait, we can all grab something after the meeting. Then a local Afro-Cuban group is jamming at Holden Hall—that's one of the dorms. Last time they played, they let me sit in on conga drum."

"Why, Ned," George said, "I didn't know you were a drummer."

Ned gave her an impish grin. "If you'd been there

and heard me, you'd know I'm not. I had a lot of fun pretending, though."

"What about the Rai Rebels?" Bess asked. "I can't wait to hear them live."

"Don't worry, you will. They're part of the concerts on Saturday and Sunday on the quad," Ned told her. "And I think they're playing at the dance Saturday night, too."

Bess's eyes sparkled with anticipation. The weekend had barely started, but Nancy could see that for Bess, it was already a great success.

The student center was a big old-fashioned building that had once been the president's mansion. They pushed through the carved oak doors and paused to look around. The entrance hall was two stories high, with wood-paneled walls and tall, narrow stained-glass windows. The row of computer terminals against one wall looked out of place in such an antique setting.

The aroma of french fries and hamburgers drifted over from a grill at the far end of the hall. Ned looked past Nancy and waved to someone at one of the tables set up in the center of the room.

Nancy turned. A tall, muscular guy with light brown hair and a deep tan was smiling and waving back. On his T-shirt was a blindingly bright graphic of a surfer and the words Bondi Beach.

Nancy remembered that Bondi Beach was a famous surfing spot in Australia. Aha! she thought. That must be Cyril.

"Hey, Cyril," Ned called. "Come meet our visitors."

After the introductions, Bess asked, "Why don't you have more of an accent?"

George winced and nudged Bess with her elbow. Bess gave her an injured look, then added, "I'm sorry, I didn't mean to offend you."

Cyril grinned. "Offend me, Bess? Not a bit of it," he replied. "I've a fair dinkum accent. But I syve it for when I'm wif me mytes. If Mel Gibson can sound like he's from Kansas City, why can't I?"

"Hello. You must be Ned's friends from River Heights," a soft voice said.

"Oh, hi, Joann," Ned said to a thin girl with straight short black hair. "Meet Nancy, Bess, and George. George, Joann offered to put you up."

"Great," George said. "I really appreciate it."

"Joann? Is that an Asian name?" Bess wondered out loud. George nudged her again. Bess wrinkled her nose at her.

The girl gave her a brief smile. "Oh, no," she said. "At home I am Xiao Yan. When I came here to study, I decided to call myself by an American name that would be easier for people to say. I chose Joann because it sounded so familiar. Do you like it?"

"Um, sure," Bess said. Her cheeks turned pink.

Nancy could see that Bess felt embarrassed about asking Joann about her name. "*Joann's* a nice name," she said, jumping in. "But I like *Xiao Yan,* too. Did I say it right?"

"Oh, yes, very good," Joann said. She looked over at George. "Would you like to go by my room now? You could drop off your things."

Ned broke off his conversation with Cyril. "Why don't you wait a little," he suggested, glancing at his watch. "Penny and Dina said they'd come by to meet Bess and Nancy. Bess, you're staying with Penny, and Nancy's with Dina. Once they get here, we can work out how to link up later."

"I hope Dina's okay," Cyril said. "When I saw her a couple of hours ago, she seemed on edge."

"The campaign's probably getting on her nerves," Ned told him. He turned to Nancy. "Dina's the club's treasurer now and is running to succeed Cyril as president of the International Friendship Club. It looks like a tight race."

Cyril laughed. "Times do change. Last year no one wanted to be president. Criselda, the outgoing president, almost begged me to stand for office. I was elected by a vote of twenty-one to zero. But here we are now with two candidates and everyone else choosing sides. It makes things lively, but I do wish people didn't take it quite so seriously."

"Who is Dina running against?" asked Nancy.

"A bloke named Vlad Miuskin," Cyril replied. "Very serious, very intense.He's from Rethalstan, in Eastern

Europe. Same part of the world as Dina, as a matter of fact. She's from Gorvonia, right next door."

"That's quite a coincidence," George remarked.

"No coincidence at all," Cyril told her. "Their countries have been going at it hammer and tongs for generations. When Vlad found out a Gorvonian might be the next IFC president, he decided to try for it himself. Or maybe it was the other way around."

"People should try harder to get along with one another," Joann said. "Even if they are from countries that disagree. Why else have an International Friendship Club?"

"Maybe *you* should run for president of the club, Joann," Bess suggested.

Joann gave her a look of alarm. "Oh, no," she gasped. "That would not do. I am no politician."

"I'm not, either," Cyril joked. "My record proves that. Seriously, Joann, you should think about standing for election. It would do the IFC a world of good to have you on the board."

"You are kind to say this," Joann murmured. "Please excuse me. There is something I must do."

Nancy watched Joann cross over to the nearest computer terminal a few feet away. She wondered why the girl had reacted so strongly to Bess's suggestion. Was it something from her culture that made her nervous about making herself stand out? Or maybe she was simply very shy.

Joann typed briefly, not bothering to sit. Nancy saw what looked like an e-mail program come up on the monitor. Joann stared at the screen. Suddenly she clutched the computer shelf with both hands. The blood drained from her face, and she swayed forward. As her knees gave way, she started to slump to the floor.

2

Suspended Animation

Nancy dashed over to Joann's side. She caught the girl an instant before her forehead struck the edge of the computer shelf.

"Are you okay?" Nancy asked, holding Joann up by the shoulders. "Did you hurt yourself?"

Joann took a deep breath. She straightened up and shook her head. "No, it is . . . I am fine. Please, it is nothing."

"Sit down," Nancy urged her and helped her to sit on the chair at the computer. "Bess, get her some water, please."

The others had gathered around her and Joann as Bess ran off for a glass of water.

"What's wrong?" Ned demanded. "Anything I can do to help?"

"Joann felt faint," Nancy told him.

"I am sorry," Joann whispered. She raised her head to look at Ned. "I have had some bad news, that is all."

"Is someone back home ill?" Cyril asked sympathetically.

"No, no, nothing like that," Joann said quickly. She shook her head, and a dizzy expression came over her face.

"You should put your head between your knees," Nancy said, and took the glass of water that Bess had brought.

Ned caught Nancy's gaze and raised his eyebrows. Nancy briefly shook her head, indicating that Joann would probably find it easier to talk to just one person. The others moved off.

"What's the matter, Joann?" Nancy asked.

Joann stared past Nancy into the distance. After a short silence she said, "My country is having very bad troubles with the economy. It is only temporary, I am sure. We are hard-working people. But I am in America on a government scholarship."

"Uh-oh," Nancy murmured. She could guess where this was heading.

Joann nodded. "Yes. Last week I learned that all programs to pay for study in other countries have been suspended. That means I have no more financial aid."

"That's terrible," Nancy said. "What are you going to do? Can your family help out, just until the situation gets better?"

"They would like to," Joann said. Tears glistened in her eyes. "You understand, we are not wealthy people, but they would do all they could. But now, because of the crisis, no one is allowed to send money out of the country."

"That's not fair," Nancy said indignantly.

Joann gave a fatalistic shrug. "When there is a crisis, many things happen that are not fair. The problems of one little student in far-off America do not count for much. Now today the college registrar sends me an e-mail. I am suspended until I have paid the next installment on my bills."

Nancy's jaw dropped. "They're kicking you out of college? That's ridiculous. You're not to blame if the economy of your country goes sour. Can't you file an appeal?"

"They are right. I owe the money and I cannot pay," Joann said. "But that is not the worst. If I am not enrolled as a student, I will lose my visa. I will have to leave the United States without my degree. After such a failure the authorities at home will never allow me to return."

"I wonder if the International Friendship Club could help you," Nancy said. "What if Cyril spoke to somebody in the college administration? Once people hear about your situation, they're bound to find a way to take care of it."

She looked around. George and Bess were chatting

13

with a redheaded girl in white jeans and a turquoise Indian print top. A few feet away Ned and Cyril were having their own conversation. Nancy waved for them to come over.

"What's up?" Cyril asked Joann. "You've had quite a turn."

Joann gave Nancy an imploring look. Nancy realized she didn't want to explain it all again. She gave the two guys a quick summary of Joann's plight.

Cyril made a disgusted noise. "Bureaucrats!" he said. "Same the world over, aren't they? Still, not to worry. Enjoy the festival. Try not to think about their idiotic doings. Come Monday we'll see if we can't pound some common sense into their heads."

"Thank you, Cyril," Joann said. "You're very sweet. I must write an e-mail to my parents. I am worried about them, and I know they must be worried about me."

"Steering committee at six," Cyril reminded her. "If you're up for it, that is. You could probably solve a couple of computer problems that have popped up. Don't worry, though. If you can't make it, I'll ask Lance to see what he can do."

Ned winked at Nancy. "Cyril's one of those guys who thinks computers are brainy typewriters with mysterious stuff inside," he kidded. "It's a good thing he's got people like Joann and this Lance to turn to when something goes wrong."

Joann got to her feet. Some color had come back to her cheeks. Nancy thought she was recovering.

"Of course I'll be at the meeting," Joann told Cyril. "We have so many details to take care of."

As George, Bess, and the girl with red hair joined them, Joann said, "I'm going to e-mail my parents now. As soon as you are ready to go to my room, please tell me, George." George nodded.

"Nancy, this is Penny," Bess announced. "I'm staying in her room. She's organizing a Worldbeat picnic tomorrow, as part of the festival. Isn't that neat?"

"It sounds like fun," Nancy replied, giving Penny a friendly smile.

"Oh, I hope so," Penny said. "I'm pretty nervous. I've never done anything like this before."

"Don't worry," Cyril told her. "None of the people who come have ever been to anything like this, either. As long as the food is exotic, they're bound to think it's a success."

"But what counts as exotic these days?" George wondered. "Even the food court at the River Heights mall has everything from French crêpes to Thai chicken."

"And it's all made from the same brand of cardboard," Nancy joked.

"Oh, come on, Nancy," Bess protested. "You have to admit it's the very *best* cardboard."

"Everything at the picnic will be homemade, from authentic recipes," Penny told them. "How about you guys? Would you like to contribute a dish?"

15

"I do a cool tossed salad," George said with a straight face. "The secret's in knowing how to toss it."

Penny laughed. "If I'm really desperate, I'll get in touch with you," she promised. She looked toward the entrance and waved. "Lance, over here!"

Lance was a guy of medium height with a squarish face and neatly trimmed blond hair. He was wearing freshly pressed khaki slacks and a blue polo shirt with a designer logo embroidered on the chest.

"Hey, look what I've got," he said to Penny. He reached into a supple brown leather messenger bag and pulled out a colorful brochure. Nancy caught a glimpse of the words "Bike Adventure."

"Lance, these are Ned's friends from River Heights," Penny said. "Bess, George, and Nancy."

"Oh, hi," Lance said. Nancy noticed he didn't ask who went with which name. "Have you girls made plans for the summer? The IFC's organizing a really super bike trip around Eastern Europe. You'd have a wonderful time. Beautiful scenery, good company, healthy exercise . . . how can you lose? Here—all the information's in here."

He handed each of them a brochure and added, "If you think you might want to go but you're not positive, fill out the form anyway and give me a deposit. That way you're sure of a place. And if you change your mind before the first of June, you get your money back."

"It sounds like fun," George said. "How many people have signed up so far?"

"Almost two dozen," Penny replied. "Isn't that great? And that was even before we got the brochure. I can't wait for summer!"

"Come by our booth at the fair tomorrow," Lance said. "We can give you a lot more information and answer any questions you have. By the end of next week you can visit our Web site, too. We'll have hyperlinks to all kinds of international stuff—music, culture, festivals, you name it."

"Lance is the official IFC Webmaster," Penny announced proudly. She put an arm through his.

"Cool," Nancy said. She looked around. Ned and Cyril had gone over to a table to study some papers. A guy with broad shoulders and thick dark hair walked up to them. Turning his back on Ned, he started talking intently to Cyril.

Ned met Nancy's gaze. He rolled his eyes, then crossed over to her. "Politics," he snorted. "I guess it gives people something to worry about."

"Who's that?" Nancy asked. "No, wait, let me guess. The guy Cyril mentioned, who's running for IFC president?"

"Good work," Ned replied. "Yeah, that's Vlad. His latest thing is that Dina is using unfair tactics against him. He just told Cyril he should disqualify her from running."

"Can Cyril do that?" Nancy asked, surprised.

Ned shrugged. "Beats me. I never read the club by-laws. But even if he could, I can't see him doing it. Not unless the person did something pretty far out of line."

"I don't get it," Nancy said. "Why is the race so bitter? Is it so important who wins? Does the head of the club have a lot of power on campus?"

"Oh, sure," Ned said with a laugh. "The IFC president ranks right up there with the assistant manager of the freshman rugby team."

George, who had heard just the last of the sentence, said, "Oh, does Emerson have a rugby team? Are they playing this weekend? I'd love to watch a game. I've never seen one, except on the Sports Channel."

"Sorry, George," Ned replied, grinning. "No rugby team. I think Cyril tried to organize one last year, but he couldn't scrounge up enough players or anyone to play against."

"So you're saying nobody much cares who the new president of the IFC is," Nancy said.

"Nobody but Vlad and Dina," Ned said. "They seem to care a lot. For most of the club members, all that matters is to get someone who'll do a good job. If you ask me, either of them would do that."

Bess, who had been looking around, asked, "What's the story? Are we going to hang here a while longer? Because if we are, I think I'll get a slice of pizza."

"We're waiting for Dina," Ned told her. "As soon as she shows up, we can head over to the dorm and drop off your stuff. But, hey, if you're hungry, go ahead, enjoy."

"Anybody else?" Bess asked. They all shook their heads.

The big oak entrance door was flung open with a bang just then. A girl with short brown hair rushed in. Her face was red and her jaw was clenched. She scanned the crowd. Her eyes passed quickly over the group around Nancy, then when they reached Cyril and Vlad, her body stiffened.

Three long, quick strides carried her to where the two guys were standing. She lifted her right hand, in which she had clenched a crumpled sheet of paper and waved it in Vlad's face.

"You worm!" she said loudly. "Filthy Rethal worm!"

Cyril put his hand on her shoulder. "Now, now," he said. "Draw it mild."

The girl brushed away his hand and took another step toward Vlad. She pushed her face forward until it was only inches from his.

"You will retract this," she declared angrily. "At once, in public, and in full. If not, I will make sure you regret it for the rest of your miserable life!"

She whirled around and snatched a cup half-full of water off the nearest table. Just as she flung the contents at Vlad, Cyril took a step forward. The water hit him right in the face.

3

Hearts and Daggers

Cyril wiped the water off his face. Nancy grabbed a handful of paper napkins and ran to give them to him. The shocked silence was broken by somebody's nervous giggle.

The girl who had thrown the water took in a quick breath and clapped her hand over her open mouth. "Oh, Cyril," she blurted out. "I am so sorry! I didn't mean—"

"That's all right, Dina," Cyril said. "I was planning to take a shower this week anyway."

The quip wasn't that funny, but it broke the tension. People around the room laughed. Nancy noticed that neither Vlad nor Dina joined in.

"What were you so upset over?" Cyril continued.

Dina's face, which had turned pale after she threw

the water, flushed again. "This . . . this garbage!" she said, waving the piece of paper.

Cyril took the paper from her and scanned it. Nancy peered over his shoulder. The paper was a printout of an e-mail message.

BCC: <dina14@emerson.edu>
From: Friends of International Friendship <fif@fif.org>
Subj: Urgent! Alert!!!

   To all who favor International Friendship: The treasurer of the Emerson College International Friendship Club secretly supports terrorist organizations based in GORVONIA and backed by the outlaw regime in power there. YOUR MONEY has been stolen to help these hooligans commit dreadful crimes against the peaceful citizens of neighboring Rethalstan. . . .

"A nasty bit of work," Cyril said. "Vlad, is this your doing?" He passed the paper to Vlad, who scanned it quickly.

"Even to ask me such a question is an insult," Vlad declared, sticking his chin out. He gave the paper back to Cyril. "I have never seen that before. But now I read it, I wonder if it is true."

"You *gorabshik!*" Dina hissed.

Nancy had never heard the word before, but she could tell from Dina's tone that it was not a compliment.

Penny put an arm around Dina's shoulders and led her a few feet away. Vlad made a move to follow, but Cyril blocked his path and started talking to him in an undertone.

Ned took the printout from Cyril's hand and walked over to the window to read it. Nancy joined him. As she passed Bess and George, she noticed Lance pointing to the bike trip brochure and talking to them earnestly.

"Who are these 'Friends of International Friendship'?" Nancy asked Ned. "Have you ever heard of them?"

Ned shook his head. "Nope. Sounds phony to me." He pointed to the lines of small print at the bottom. "According to the header info, this came through the college's anonymous server. That means whoever sent it had to have access to the campus LAN. That stands for Local Area Network."

"And whoever sent it had to know Dina's e-mail address," Nancy said. "Is there any way to tell who else got this?"

"I doubt it," Ned replied. "The sender kept the list of recipients blind. That's what those letters BCC mean. Let's check my mailbox."

Nancy followed him over to a computer terminal and waited while he typed in his user name and password.

A list of a dozen e-mail messages appeared on the

screen. Ned tapped one with his forefinger. "There it is," he said. *"Urgent! Alert!!!* And if it came to me, it's a safe bet that everyone in the IFC got one."

"And who knows who else?" Nancy added. "But we should make sure about that. If so, it's an important clue. It proves that the poison-pen writer got his hands on a copy of the IFC membership list. How easy would that be to do?"

"A new list was sent out to all the members at the start of the semester," Ned replied. "But I just thought of something. Penny switched to a new e-mail address a couple of weeks ago. She was getting too much spam and garbage at her old one."

Nancy grabbed his arm. "So if she got this message, it means the sender not only has the IFC mailing list, he has the latest version of it."

Nancy looked around. Penny was still with Dina. They were talking in a confidential way. Nancy caught Penny's eye and beckoned her over. Penny said something quickly to Dina, then joined them. Nancy explained what they wanted. Just moments later they had the answer to their question. There was a copy of the e-mail from "Friends of International Friendship" in Penny's mailbox.

"Let's check one other thing," Nancy said, taking Penny's place at the keyboard. She typed in *www.fif.org* and hit Return. After a short pause a banner appeared across the top of the screen: <u>Welcome to</u>

"That means the 'From' line in the message is a phony," Ned said. "I can't say I'm surprised."

"Me either," Nancy replied. "If I were sending a poison-pen letter, I don't think I'd be dumb enough to give my real return address."

"Who would do a thing like this?" Penny wondered.

"I don't know, but we're going to try to find out," Nancy told her.

Penny looked at her with wide eyes. "That's right, you're a detective!" she exclaimed. "I forgot that. It's so lucky you're here to help."

Dina walked over to them. "What is lucky?" she demanded. "What are you doing? Has something else happened?"

"Ned and I both got that e-mail," Penny replied.

"I knew it," Dina said. "This is Vlad's doing."

"Boh!" Vlad shouted from across the room. "You probably sent it yourself. Maybe you think this is the way to win votes out of sympathy. But you will see. IFC members are too intelligent to fall for your stupid tricks."

Cyril took Vlad's arm and tugged him toward the door. "Come on, chum," he said. "Let's you and me take a walk. Everyone needs a chance to cool off. We'll have to pull together if we're going to make the festival a success."

As Cyril and Vlad left, Ned glanced at his watch.

24

"Uh-oh," he said. "I just remembered. I left some papers in my room. I have to go get them before the steering committee meeting at six. Penny, would you mind taking charge of Nancy, George, and Bess for a little while?"

"No problem," Penny said cheerfully. "Dina? Joann? Let's take our guests by the dorm and show them where they'll be staying."

"The meeting's in the common room on the ground floor of Centennial," Ned added to Nancy. He sounded apologetic. "That's the dorm you're in. After you get settled, come downstairs and find us."

"Sure, Nickerson," Nancy said, wrinkling her nose at him. "Don't worry about us. We can take care of ourselves."

Nancy and her friends grabbed their knapsacks and followed Penny, Joann, and Dina out of the student center. On the walk across campus, both Joann and Dina were silent and preoccupied. After a couple of tries at talking to them, George and Bess joined Nancy and Penny.

"How do you like it here at Emerson, Penny?" asked Bess.

"Oh, I love it," Penny responded. "It's been such an education for me, especially meeting other kids from all over the world. Do you know, we have students here from practically every state and from over thirty other countries? It's almost like having a little UN, right on campus."

25

"How about you?" George asked. "Where are you from?"

Penny made a funny face. "I grew up in a little town in Indiana," she said. "Miles from anyplace you've heard of. It was kind of closed in. I knew all the kids in my high school class since kindergarten, and four of them were some kind of cousin."

"George and I are cousins," Bess remarked.

Penny blushed. "Don't get me wrong, I like my cousins—most of them, anyway. There are a couple I could do without."

George laughed. "I think everybody feels that way now and then," she said with a pointed look at Bess.

Bess just gave her a very sweet smile.

"I didn't mean to start anything between you two," Penny said with a smile. "They say old friends are the best. Maybe so, but it's great to meet new people, too. And you can imagine what it was like for me, getting to know kids from Brazil and India and different countries in Africa—all over. That's why I love being in the IFC."

Nancy looked around. Joann and Dina were a dozen feet behind, walking separately. Lowering her voice, Nancy asked Penny, "What was all that just now?"

"With Vlad and Dina, you mean?" Penny replied. "I *hate* politics. It makes people so mean sometimes. Dina and Vlad are both pretty nice when you get them by themselves. But they've been going at it like cats and dogs ever since they met, all because their countries don't get along. That is *so* sick! And now that they're both running for president of the club, it's a hundred times worse."

"Oh, well," George said. "It's not for long. The election's pretty soon, isn't it?"

Penny shook her head. "Two weeks from now. But you don't understand. So many people are taking sides. It doesn't matter who wins. A lot of the kids who supported the loser will probably drop out. Or they'll stay around and make things so unpleasant that the rest of us will drop out."

"That's terrible," Bess said. "What about people like you, who only want what's best for the club? Can't you do anything?"

"We're trying," Penny said with a sad smile. "Maybe if we all work on making the festival a big success, we'll learn to get along, in spite of our differences. I hope so, anyway."

"So do I," Bess said. "I think international friendship is so important. And worldbeat rules!"

Centennial Hall was a three-story building of redbrick, with ivy climbing up the walls. The white pillars flanking the front steps gave it a colonial look.

Inside, Penny paused and pointed to the room on the left. "That's the common room," she said. "Where the steering committee will be meeting."

Nancy glanced through the doorway. The room

looked impressive but comfortable. The walls were paneled in dark wood. At the far end, over a brick fireplace with a carved wooden mantel, was a large painting of a man with a white beard, wearing academic robes. Couches and easy chairs were scattered around the room. About half were occupied by students who were reading or napping with open books on their laps. One guy was stretched out on a couch with his shoes off, snoring loudly.

"It looks nice," George said. "Is this where you usually study?"

"Most of the time I go to the library," Penny replied. "It's not as cozy there, so it's easier to stay awake."

Dina and Joann caught up to them in time to hear this. Joann gave a small smile. "After twenty pages of my psych text, it is hard to stay awake anywhere," she said.

"You should try economics," Dina told her. "Five pages is better than any sleeping pill."

At the back of the entrance hall a wide stairway led to the upper floors. When the girls reached the second floor, Penny said, "Bess, we're down this way. Room One Fourteen."

"And we are in the other direction, in One Fifty-one," Joann said to George.

Nancy made a mental note of the two room numbers, then gave Dina a querying look.

"Another flight," Dina said. "Sorry."

At the top of the stairs Dina turned left along a narrow corridor. Each door had a whiteboard attached to it, with the names of the occupants at the top and a marker dangling from a string. Nancy noted some of the messages on the boards as she walked past.

"Lynn—meet at library." "Hi, Kevin, catch you later, Pat." "HELP—e-mail me calc assignment ASAP, Josie."

Up ahead, Dina came to a sudden stop next to one of the doors. The stiff way she was holding her shoulders alerted Nancy that something was wrong. Nancy walked faster, then broke into a run.

Dina was staring at her whiteboard. Below her name was a crude drawing of a heart with a dagger sticking through it.

4

Threats and Menaces

As Dina stared at the ominous drawing, she was feeling around in her shoulder bag. Pulling out a tissue, she swiped it across the whiteboard.

"Wait!" Nancy started to say. Too late. Dina had already wiped away the evidence.

Nancy quickly closed her eyes and tried to visualize the drawing. Had there been anything unusual about it? It seemed to her that the point of the dagger was unfinished. Maybe the perpetrator had been interrupted while drawing it.

"This time I *know* Vlad is guilty," Dina asserted.

Nancy looked at her. The girl's fists were clenched so tightly that her nails were digging into her palms. Her eyes blazed with anger.

"What makes you so sure?" Nancy asked. "That was a pretty ugly thing to find on your door, but I didn't notice any signature on it."

"Only a filthy Rethal would stoop to such a deed," Dina replied. "Who but Vlad would know what this means to me? You must understand, the heart is the sacred symbol of my homeland. To put a knife through it like that is to stab me and every Gorvonian!"

Uh-oh. Nancy realized that she was in the middle of an emotional minefield. Unless she was very careful, any step she took in any direction could result in an explosion.

"Dina?" Nancy began. "When was the last time you were at your room today?"

"An hour ago?" Dina replied. "A little more, maybe. That was when I discovered that infamous message."

"And there wasn't any drawing on your door then?" Nancy continued.

"Of course not!" Dina exclaimed. "Would I have left it there for everyone to see?"

"Hmm." Nancy rubbed the back of her neck. "And the heart symbol—is it widely known?"

Dina raised her chin. "In my part of the world, everyone knows that the heart is the Gorvonian emblem," she replied sternly.

"Oh, I'm sure they do," Nancy said hastily. "I meant here, at Emerson College. I imagine most students don't know much about Gorvonia." To herself she added, Or even know it exists.

"This is so," Dina said. "I do what I can to educate them. Last semester I gave a slide show about the history and culture of my country."

"And you mentioned the heart symbol?" Nancy prodded.

Dina stood taller. "Of course. The first slide was the national coat of arms. Why are you asking this?"

"I was just wondering," Nancy said. "From what you say, anyone who came to your slide show would know what a horrible insult that drawing would be. Were there many people there?"

"I did not count," Dina told her with gloomy pride. "Many from the IFC, of course. Others? Well . . . this is not a place with a strong international outlook. Besides, there was a sports rally and bonfire the same night."

She took out her key and opened the door. "Please come in," she said, standing aside. "This is your home."

The room was furnished as a double, with the beds arranged in an L. An easy chair occupied one corner. A desk, against the opposite wall, held a stack of books and papers and a laptop computer. The twin windows looked out into the upper branches of an oak tree.

"Where do you want me?" Nancy asked.

"The bed on the right." Dina said in reply.

"Sure," Nancy said quickly.

"Good." Dina rummaged around on her desktop and found a set of keys. "These are for you. The girls' bathroom is down the hall to the left. I must go to the meeting. We will meet later."

Dina started toward the door, then turned back and paused. For a moment a smile lighted her face. She looked like a different person. "I am glad you are here, Nancy," she said. "I will like to share my room with you, if only for the weekend."

She left. As Nancy unpacked her clothes, she imagined what it would be like to go to college in a foreign country, far from her family and friends. Exciting, yes, but at the same time so terribly lonely.

Nancy finished unpacking and went in search of Bess and George, who were just coming up the stairs to look for her.

"How's your room?" Bess was asking George. "I bet you took the upper bunk. Penny always sleeps up top, so I lucked out. I was so afraid I'd roll over in the night and go crashing down."

"Good thing you're not a mountain climber," George said. "Once I had to sleep on a ledge that wasn't more than two feet wide, with a five-hundred-foot drop next to me."

"And you slept?" Bess demanded, wide eyed. "I would have been trembling so much, I probably would have jerked my way off the edge."

They all laughed. Then Nancy said, "Something's happened that we should look into." As they walked back to her room, she told them about the heart-

and-dagger drawing and explained what it meant.

"I think we should find out if anyone saw anything," she added. "There don't seem to be many people in the dorm at this time of day, but we might get lucky."

At that moment they heard footsteps. A guy in jeans and an Emerson College sweatshirt was coming down the hall. He gave them a friendly nod and started past to go on to the stairs.

"Could I ask you a question?" Nancy said. She introduced herself and her friends and explained that they were visiting for the weekend. "I'm staying with Dina. And when we got to her room just now, there was an ugly drawing on her door."

"The thing with a knife?" the guy asked. "Yeah, I noticed that a little while ago. Pretty creepy."

"You didn't see who made it, did you?" George asked.

"Nope. Sorry," he replied. "I've got a test in organic chem on Monday, so I've been hitting the books pretty hard. I'm just coming up for air."

"Do you remember *when* you saw the drawing?" Bess asked. "That might help us figure out who did it."

The guy grinned. "I get it—alibis and stuff, huh? Let's see . . . it's about six now . . . call it forty-five minutes ago, about five-fifteen, plus or minus fifteen minutes."

Nancy made a note of the information and thanked him. After he clattered down the stairs, she said, "That's a start. Let's fan out and knock on doors."

* * *

34

"*Nada,*" Bess said disgustedly, when the three friends reconvened at the head of the stairs half an hour later. "Zip. Zilch. Nobody home except two girls who saw and heard nothing. If you ask me, you could have sent the college marching band through here, and they wouldn't have noticed."

Nancy grinned. "Same here," she reported. "I guess almost everybody's off at the dining hall or library. How about you, George? Any luck?"

"A little," George replied. "I found one guy, Carlos. He took a shower late this afternoon, and on the way back to his room he noticed somebody standing by Dina's door. The somebody hurried away when he heard Carlos coming."

"*He?*" Nancy repeated. "Carlos was sure it was a guy? Any details? Build, hair color, clothes?"

George shook her head. "Carlos was thirty feet down the hall and his glasses were still fogged over from the shower room. He's only about eighty percent sure it was Dina's door. Still, it gives us a possible fix on the time: five-twenty. *That* he's sure about. He was expecting a call at five-thirty, so he was watching the time."

"That fits with what we know from Dina and that guy," Nancy said thoughtfully. "So anybody with an alibi for five-twenty is less of a suspect. Do we know when Vlad showed up at the student center?"

"We got there a little before five," George said. "So it

must have been about five-thirty when he came in. No help there."

"No," Nancy said. She felt a shiver run down her spine. "Two nasty incidents in one afternoon. I have a hunch they're just the beginning."

"Hey, you guys," Ned called from one flight down. "We were looking for you. Come on. Let's get something to eat."

Cyril was with Ned. So was a guy with delicate features, a dark complexion, glossy black hair, and flashing eyes.

"This is Jay Prakash, known as J. P.," Ned said. "He's coming to dinner with us. What do you say to El Taco Loco?"

"I never met a crazy taco I didn't like," George joked. "J. P., are you from India?"

"My grandparents were," J. P. replied. "But I was born and raised in Guyana. That's a very small country on the northeast coast of South America."

"I knew that," Bess announced. "It used to be a British colony, right?"

J. P. smiled. "You could say that about many parts of the world, including Cyril's homeland, Australia. But yes."

"Enough geopolitics," Cyril said. "I'm famished."

El Taco Loco was a short walk from campus. Inside, the walls were decorated with sombreros, serapes, and a mural of a cactus. Mariachi music played over the sound system. Their waitress wore a lace-trimmed peasant blouse and a long, full skirt decorated with sequin-covered bullfighters.

Nancy scanned the menu. There were the usual combination plates of enchiladas, tacos, rice and beans, and guacamole, but she spotted some more unusual dishes as well. She chose roast chicken with a spicy sauce made from bitter chocolate.

As dinner went on, she noticed that Bess was talking mostly to Cyril. George and J. P. seemed to be getting along well, too. Good. Nancy did not want her friends to feel neglected or left out when she and Ned took some time for themselves.

"Our steering committee meeting got pretty lively," Ned said in a low voice. "I'm worried about Dina. I've never seen her so on edge."

"I'm not surprised," Nancy replied. She told him about the drawing on Dina's door and what she, George, and Bess had found out.

Ned rubbed his chin. "Hmm . . . it doesn't have to be Vlad, you know. The way people are choosing sides in this IFC election, one of Vlad's supporters could have gotten carried away."

"That's what worries me most," Nancy replied. "And if some of those who support Dina decide to retaliate, you could end up with a real mess."

* * *

37

Cyril finished eating and left before the others. He wanted to make sure everything was ready for the music that evening. When Nancy and the others got to Holden Hall, they found the lounge already crowded. Early arrivals had grabbed the couches and chairs around three sides of the room. Everyone else was standing or on pillows on the floor. An area in front of the musicians had been left clear for dancing.

"So, Nickerson," Nancy said mischievously, "do we get to hear you on conga tonight?"

"Sure, Drew," Ned replied. "And how about I tell Jorge, the band leader, to call you up as a guest vocalist?"

"You do, and you'll be wearing that conga drum as a necklace," Nancy threatened.

Ned looked ready to try to top her, but at that moment the band filed in. Cyril picked up a mike and welcomed the crowd to the Emerson College Worldbeat Festival and gave a quick rundown of the weekend's events.

"But that's enough from me," he concluded. "Now, *party on!*"

After three sharp taps on the bongo, the two guitarists started the infectious rhythm of a mambo. As the trumpeter launched into the melody, three couples took the dance floor. The rest of the room clapped and swayed in time to the music.

A slow number brought most of the crowd to the dance floor. Nancy had almost forgotten how much she loved dancing with Ned. Why didn't they do it more often? When the music ended, everyone cheered. Not waiting for the applause to die down, the grinning musicians went into a cha-cha.

"Do you know how to dance to this?" Ned asked.

"I think I saw a lesson on TV once," Nancy replied.

"Uh-huh. I don't know, either," Ned said. "But, hey, who's watching? Come on, let's try."

As she and Ned cha-cha'ed around the room, Nancy kept an eye out for her friends. She spotted George on the sidelines, talking to J. P. A moment later Bess and Cyril swept past. What they were doing looked more like a tango than the cha-cha, but they were obviously having fun. So were all the rest of the kids in the room.

Oops—*almost* all. Dina was standing alone at the side of the room, wearing a glum expression. As Nancy watched, a guy went up to her and said something. Dina shook her head, without even looking at him. He shrugged and went away.

For the rest of the evening Nancy tried to put Dina out of her mind and enjoy her time with Ned. It was hard. She kept finding herself thinking of new questions about the e-mail and the drawing. She was tense, too, half-expecting something else to happen. She was almost glad when the music ended and the crowd started to drift away.

Ned walked her back to Dina's dorm. After a few minutes of quiet closeness, he went on to his frat house and she went upstairs. Dina was already in bed with her eyes closed. Nancy changed into her pajamas and went down the hall to wash up and brush her teeth.

Just as she returned to the room, the phone rang.

Dina sprang up. It was almost as if she had been waiting for something like this. She pressed the button that turned on the speakerphone.

"This is a friendly warning," a whispery voice said. "If you know what's good for you, you will quit the race for IFC president. If you don't, you could get hurt. Pay attention, or else."

5

Trouble at the Bazaar

"Who is this?" Dina demanded. "What do you want?"

"Never mind who I am. You have been warned."

The voice fell silent. Just before the click of the hangup, Nancy heard what sounded like a truck starting up.

Dina reached for the button to turn off the phone. She hit it so fiercely that the handset jumped off the console and dangled from its cord. She put the handset back, then buried her face in her hands.

Nancy went over and put a comforting hand on her shoulder. "That was scary," she said.

Dina looked up at her. "How can someone be so mean?" she wondered. "Night after night . . . I will never sleep now."

"You've had calls like that before?" Nancy asked.

"Oh, yes," Dina replied. "Three—no, four times. The first time he said nothing. Just silence. I thought it was a mistake, or maybe a nut. But, no, it is filthy politics."

"Did the voice sound familiar?" Nancy probed. "Or the accent?"

Dina hesitated. "Well, no. But is it hard to guess who would do such a thing? Obviously Vlad or one of his henchmen."

Nancy was silent. Dina might be right, of course. But was it a coincidence that the call had come at the very moment Nancy returned to the room? It was almost as if the caller wanted to be sure Nancy heard it. Was he watching the room, either from another room down the hall or from outside? That was a frightening thought.

However, there was another possibility. What if *Dina* had set up the call? She could have signaled the caller when she heard Nancy returning to the room, then pretended to be asleep. As for a motive, she might want to prove to the IFC members how underhanded her opponent was. If so, an outsider like Nancy would make a perfect witness.

As Nancy climbed into bed, she resolved to keep an open mind until she could learn more about the case.

"What a glorious morning!" Bess exclaimed. "Cyril, did you arrange for this weather?"

"Too right I did," Cyril replied. "I ordered it specially from back home. Down Under, every day is perfect, of course, so they'd plenty to spare."

The band of friends was walking across campus after meeting for a quick breakfast in the dining hall.

"Where are we headed?" George asked.

"We've been given the quad near the gym," J. P. told her. "Most events during the day will happen there. And the dance tonight is inside the gym, so that is very convenient."

Nancy and Ned dropped back a few steps. In a low voice, Nancy told Ned about the threatening phone call and related her thoughts about it.

Ned frowned. "I don't know Vlad or Dina that well," he said. "But I'd hate to think either of them would sink to making midnight crank calls."

"*Somebody* did," Nancy pointed out. "Would you quietly ask what other IFC members did after the music last night? Maybe a bunch of them went out for food. The call came at twelve thirty-four. Anyone who is vouched for at that time is in the clear."

"I'll see what I can find out," Ned said. "But I'm not too hopeful. People who are hanging out late don't usually keep such close check on the time."

"I know," Nancy told him. "And someone could have slipped away long enough to call, without the others noticing. Still, we might get lucky. Is that where we're going?"

Up ahead was a big grassy area marked off by red wooden snow fences. Over the entrance, an arch of brightly colored helium balloons bobbed and swayed in the breeze. A hand-painted banner read, Worldbeat Festival Bazaar—Sat & Sun—Free Admission.

Booths had been set up around three sides of the lawn. A few were still vacant, but most already bustled with activity. Exhibitors hurried between the grounds and their double parked cars and vans, unloading folding tables, rolled-up banners, and cartons of merchandise.

At the far end of the lawn members of the college grounds crew were setting up a temporary stage and rows of folding chairs. Behind the stage was a green-and yellow-striped tent.

As Nancy and her friends neared the entrance, a guy wearing a yellow-and-green dashiki spotted them and came over. "So, Cyril," he said, offering his hand. "The great day arrives, eh?"

"Right on schedule," Cyril replied. "Akai, meet Ned's guests, Bess, George, and Nancy. Akai is from Nigeria. He's commander in chief of the bazaar."

"More like custodian," Akai said with a chuckle. "Excuse me for rushing off. The video monitors were delivered, but not the power cords."

"What are the monitors for?" Bess asked, after Akai left.

"We'll be showing tapes about life in different countries throughout the day," Cyril told her. "We hope they'll help promote a better understanding of the world."

Nancy saw Penny and Lance across the street. Each was carrying a stack of cartons. She pointed them out and said, "Let's give them a hand."

"Ouf! Thanks," Penny said after Nancy ran up and took the top carton. "I don't know how it is, but every few steps this stuff got heavier."

J. P. and George each took another carton from her stack, while Ned, Bess, and Cyril helped Lance.

"What have you got here, anyway?" Bess wondered.

"Dishes for the international buffet," Penny explained. "People have been preparing them at the Food Services kitchen for the last couple of days. Talk about good smells! We'll store them in the fridge at the gym, then heat them just before it's time to serve."

"We should be sure to line up early," Ned said. "The most interesting dishes are bound to run out. We don't want to miss them."

"They're *all* interesting," Penny insisted. She led them through the side door of the gym, to a well-equipped kitchen. "The college holds a lot of events here, so they need facilities to prepare food. Good thing for us. I don't know how we would have managed the buffet otherwise."

"Do you need more help?" asked Cyril.

"Not at this point," Penny said. "I'll holler if I do."

"Then I'd better see how the others are coping," Cyril said. "Lance? Ned? A word?"

Ned gave Nancy an apologetic glance and followed Cyril and Lance outside. J. P. murmured something and also left.

Penny was counting cartons as she put them in the big double-door refrigerator. "Oops," she said. "I'm two short. I'd better go check."

"Listen," Nancy said to Bess and George, once the three friends were alone. She described the menacing phone call.

"Brrr," Bess said.

"We'd better keep an eye out for more trouble," George said. "And Dina's the obvious target. Where is she?"

"I don't know," Nancy replied. "She was up before I was today. All she said when she left was that she'd see us later."

"All the IFC people are really busy," George said. "Joann was out early, too."

"Let's go look for them," Bess suggested. "We can check out the bazaar at the same time."

"Shop till you drop," George said with a teasing laugh. Bess huffed, then she laughed, too.

During the time they had been gone, the scene outside had changed dramatically. Crowds of students were browsing through the booths. From one, puffs of blue smoke perfumed the air with the aroma of exotic incense. Above another flew a banner that read Songs of the Earth. Nancy heard the sound of a high, haunting chant. She imagined a rickety bridge over a deep chasm. The lines of people crossing it sang to keep their minds off the danger they faced.

"Oh, look!" Bess gasped. She pulled Nancy and George toward a table piled high with blouses in deep, rich colors. She held up one with vertical stripes of grape and emerald green. "I want this one. No, I want them all."

George checked the label. "Pretty reasonable for pure silk," she observed. "Nancy, here's a dark blue that would look great with your hair."

"I'll think about it," Nancy said.

The girl behind the table was wearing a pale green sari with a band of gold along the edges. She said, "If you like, I will keep it for you. It would be very sad to come back and find it gone."

"Go ahead," George urged. "Get it."

"Well . . . okay," Nancy said, reaching for her wallet. Ned had once told her she looked terrific in dark blue. She would surprise him by wearing the blouse to the dance that evening.

"And I'll take this one," Bess said, handing the girl the purple and green blouse and her money. "What about you, George?"

"Maybe later," George said. "First I'd like to check out the rest of the stands."

"We are here all day today and tomorrow," the girl said. "But now is the best selection."

"I'll keep that in mind," George promised.

A little farther on, past a display of African drums, they found the booth of the International Friendship Club. Nancy didn't recognize the guy seated behind the table, but he seemed to know who she and her friends were. "Ned was here just a moment ago," he told them, with a trace of a Spanish accent.

"Oh, thanks," Nancy replied. She scanned the table. Next to a colorful poster of a medieval castle, there was a large stack of the brochures Lance had given them about the summer bike trip. Nancy couldn't recall what she had done with hers, so she picked up another copy and glanced through it.

"Turning into a pedal-pusher?" Ned asked, from just behind her shoulder.

"It does look like fun," she admitted. "The scenery's gorgeous, and it doesn't look too hilly. What do you think?"

"Lots of fresh air," Ned said. "But I'd rather see the countryside from a sporty convertible. I hope it goes over. If Lance gets enough contracts by the end of the month, he goes for free. He's here at Emerson on a big scholarship, so that's quite an incentive."

From nearby, there was a sudden burst of laughter. Nancy turned to look. Eight or ten grinning students were clustered in front of one of the video monitors. They let out another loud laugh.

Suddenly Vlad pushed through the group to the front. His face was red and his jaw was clenched. Placing himself directly in front of the monitor, he faced the others.

"This is a scandal!" he shouted. "A deliberate provocation!"

Nancy, George, Bess, and Ned hurried over. Attached to the monitor stand was a sign that read, Rethalstan: History and Culture. What the monitor showed, however, was a jerky black-and-white cartoon of a battle between cats and mice. From the quick glance Nancy caught of the screen, it looked as if the mice were winning.

6

A Switch in Time

"Would you please move out of the way?" a girl in a blue tank top said to Vlad. "We're watching the cartoon."

"Yeah, what's your problem, fella?" a guy with long sideburns and a single earring added. "Lost your sense of humor?"

"This is not funny!" Vlad exclaimed. "As a Rethal, I must protest. This is an insult to my motherland!"

George edged past Vlad and hit Stop on the VCR.

"Hey!" the girl in the tank top said. "Turn it back on."

"Wait a minute," Nancy said firmly. "You don't understand. This monitor was supposed to be showing a tape about this guy's country, Rethalstan. Somebody put the wrong one on. You can see why he's upset."

"We'll show the cartoon on another monitor," Ned added. "Just let us straighten this out."

Muttering, the spectators started drifting away. Nancy ejected the videocassette and studied it. The hand-printed label read, Rethalstan: Hist & Cult.

Vlad was peering over Nancy's shoulder. "That is a crude forgery!" he blurted out. "It is not the tape I gave to Akai yesterday. Someone put this in its place. Someone who means to mock Rethalstan and the Rethal people."

Word of the incident had apparently spread. Cyril and Akai hurried over to join them. "What now?" Cyril asked.

Nancy told them about the substituted tape.

"I don't get it," Akai said, worried. "I loaded that tape in the VCR myself, just fifteen minutes ago. How could somebody switch it for another one?"

"The switch must have happened earlier," Nancy replied. "Where was the tape before you loaded it?"

Akai pointed toward the IFC booth. "Back there with the others, in a shopping bag," he told her. "I brought them over from my room this morning."

"Did you leave them unguarded?" Bess asked.

"Well, sure," Akai said. The question seemed to surprise him. "Who'd want to take them? We're talking about videotapes, not the crown jewels."

"Besides," Cyril pointed out, "there's been one or two of our members at the booth the whole time since the bazaar opened."

"Let's take a look," George suggested.

The IFC booth was just a few steps away. The guy they had met a few minutes earlier was deep in conversation in rapidfire Spanish with an older man wearing the black and silver costume of a Mexican cowboy. He gave them a bright smile and a wave.

J. P. was talking to a girl with a Caribbean lilt in her voice. "What is the matter, guys?" he asked the group when he noticed their expressions.

Ned told him about the switched video. "Were you here at the booth?" he added.

"In and out, like a dozen others," J. P. told him. "Are you sure the switch took place here?"

Nancy spotted a white shopping bag in the far corner of the booth. There were still six or eight videocassettes inside.

Akai joined her. "You see? Each one is labeled. I could not make a mistake."

"How did you decide which ones to play first?" Nancy asked.

"We made up a schedule," he replied, showing her his clipboard. "At any time we wanted tapes from different parts of the world to be playing."

Nancy glanced at the paper. One of the entries in the first group was Rethalstan: Hist & Cult.

She straightened up and looked around. *If the switch took place here, the culprit had to act quickly, without drawing attention. It would take just a mo-*

ment to slip a new tape from inside a backpack or under a shirt and drop it in the shopping bag. But what to do with the real tape about Rethalstan? Take it away? Or simply hide it? That would be a lot safer and less obvious.

Next to the bag of videotapes was a carton of pamphlets about UNICEF. Nancy opened it. Some of the pamphlets were scattered sideways. She lifted them. Underneath was a videotape labeled, *Rethalstan, History and Culture*. She picked it up and showed it to the others.

"That is it!" Vlad exclaimed. "That is the one I made. Look, you see I make the *s* different, with straight lines instead of curves. That is the custom in my country."

"That's not all," George said. "The wording is different. On your tape, *history and culture* aren't abbreviated."

"But they are on the printed schedule," Nancy pointed out.

Ned stared at her. "So whoever did the substitution had to have access to the schedule."

"It looks that way," Nancy replied. "Akai—?"

"I see where you are going," Akai said, obviously upset. "We did not try to keep it secret, but there was no reason to make it public, either. I had a copy, of course."

"So did I," Cyril offered. "And the others on the steering committee—Vlad, Lance, Penny, Criselda, Joann . . ."

"And Dina," Vlad said bitterly. "Do not forget Dina.

53

Who is more likely to spread slander about Rethalstan than a Gorvonian? Already she accuses me of this and that. Isn't it obvious?"

"Where *is* Dina?" Bess asked. "I haven't seen her all morning."

"She went to pick up some of the musicians at the airport," Cyril said. "She should have been back by now, though."

From the direction of the stage, there was a brief ear-piercing blast of feedback. Nancy looked. A Mexican mariachi band was filing out of the tent at the rear and lining up before the mikes. One of the musicians was the man in the black-and-silver outfit she had noticed earlier at the IFC booth. He had a bass guitar the size of a cello strapped around his neck. It looked big enough to topple him forward.

The guitars began a fast rhythmic strum. The crowd of students started moving toward the stage. After the trumpeter played a descending melody that was clearly an intro, the others in the band leaned toward the mikes to launch into the verse of the song. Nancy couldn't make out the words, but some in the audience sang along.

Ned moved closer to Nancy and murmured into her ear, "If Dina's been away all morning, how could she switch those tapes?"

"Good question," Nancy replied. "An accomplice?"

Ned knitted his brow. "Could be, but why take that

chance? The more people who know a secret, the less a secret it is."

"Who else has a motive, though?" Nancy wondered.

"What about Vlad?" Ned said. "If he can make people think Dina's pulling dirty tricks on him, maybe they'll vote for him in the IFC election."

"He did just happen to be right there when the tape started," Nancy recalled. "A coincidence?"

The first song ended. As the applause died down, the mariachi group went into another number. It sounded very familiar, but Nancy couldn't imagine how she knew it. She didn't hear much Mexican music. Then she burst out laughing. It was an oldie standard called "My Way," translated into Spanish and played with a Latin rhythm. This was really world music.

As the mariachi band continued, Nancy studied the crowd. George and Bess were a few feet away, standing with J. P. and Cyril. Cyril had his electronic organizer out and was frowning at the tiny screen. He turned and said something to J. P., then the two of them walked away. Bess noticed and murmured to George, who gave a shrug.

Near the IFC booth, Lance stood next to a girl with short brown hair. He was showing her the brochure for the European bike trip and talking eagerly. The girl looked as if she wanted to escape. After a few moments she took a brochure, smiled, and walked away quickly.

Lance's face fell. Then he picked up another brochure and looked around for someone else to approach.

In a fenced-off area to the left of the stage, a crew was putting up tables and chairs for the international buffet lunch. They had lined up three long tables end to end and were starting to set out metal chafing dishes for serving hot food. Penny watched from the sidelines, shifting nervously from foot to foot.

Nancy glanced over her shoulder. Dina had just come through the entrance. The people with her were carrying instrument cases. Nancy thought she recognized a couple of them from the photo on the cover of the Rai Rebels CD. This was definitely going to make Bess's weekend.

A fast, lively piece that got everyone up and dancing brought the mariachi music to an end. Cyril appeared onstage and took one of the mikes. When the applause died down, he said, "We'll have more music from around the world throughout the day. Los Amigos will be back, along with groups from Algeria, Indonesia, Brazil . . . And don't forget the dance tonight in the gym, and the gala concert tomorrow afternoon."

Penny waved her arms wildly. Cyril saw her and added, "*And* the super international buffet, which will be starting in just a few minutes from now. Better buy your tickets. You don't want to miss this chance to try delicious authentic specialties from all over."

"I bet Penny could use some help setting up," Ned

said. "And the sooner it's done, the sooner we get to sample the food."

They collected George and Bess and went inside to the gym kitchen. Half a dozen IFC members were already helping. Dina and Vlad were among them. They carefully avoided even a glance at each other.

Penny directed people to transfer the foil-covered metal serving dishes from the warming oven to wheeled carts. Each dish had a printed card saying who had prepared it, what country it was from, and what it was.

As Vlad was carrying a tray to the nearest cart, the card that went with it fluttered to the floor.

"Oh, please," Penny gasped as he picked it up. "Don't get the cards mixed up, whatever you do! I'd never get them straight!"

"Let everybody guess," a girl with a brown ponytail said. "Turn it into a contest."

"You could call it 'Name That Dish,' " J. P. added.

"Or how about, 'Who Wants to Have His Stomach Pumped?' " a guy in baggy jeans and a torn T-shirt contributed.

"That's enough of that," Penny snapped. "People worked hard cooking something special from their homelands. They deserve thanks, not sick jokes."

"Well, ex-cu-u-se me!" the guy muttered.

By the time they finished setting up the buffet, a line had formed outside the fence. Lance was at a little table, selling tickets. The girl ahead of Nancy handed him a twenty-dollar bill.

"Do you have anything smaller?" Lance asked, as he rummaged through his metal cashbox. The girl shook her head.

Nancy found four five-dollar bills in her wallet. "Here, Lance," she said. "Four, please."

"Thanks. That helps." He passed over the tickets, gave the girl her change, and put the twenty in a manila envelope tucked under the box. Noticing Nancy's glance, he said, "I put the bigger bills in the envelope so I won't mess up making change."

"Good idea," Nancy said.

J. P. and Cyril were at the back of the line. As Nancy, Ned, George, and Bess joined them, the line started moving.

"Be sure to take some of Dina's goulash," Cyril advised them. "It should be something special."

"And don't miss Vlad's stuffed squash," J. P. said. "It's made with pine nuts and wild mushrooms."

Nancy and her friends filled their plates with a wide assortment of foods and joined Cyril and J. P. at a big circular table.

"I wonder where Joann is," Nancy said, glancing around. "I haven't seen her all day."

"I have," Bess said. "She has a booth where she's selling beautiful carved teak animals. You should take a look after lunch."

"I will," Nancy promised. She studied her plate and decided to try the stuffed squash. She took a bite, but it was so salty she couldn't swallow.

"Did anyone . . . ?" she started to ask.

George was making a strange face. "Watch out for the goulash," she gasped. "It's practically straight sugar."

At the next table a girl made a loud gagging noise. Clapping a hand over her mouth, she jumped up, over-turning her chair, and ran toward the entrance.

7

Sugar and Spice

People watched the girl run out, then looked dubiously at their plates. Here and there, others got to their feet. The hubbub of voices rose in volume and pitch.

"We'd better do something, quick," Nancy said grimly. "Before there's a panic."

Cyril took in the situation instantly. He jumped up onto his chair and stretched both arms over his head.

"Can I have your attention?" he shouted. "Quiet, please. I have an important announcement."

Some in the crowd kept talking urgently. Others shushed them. Gradually a silence fell.

"Somebody has played a very nasty practical joke," Cyril continued. "It seems that one or two of the dishes we're serving have been deliberately ruined."

"That stew!" someone yelled. "It tastes terrible!"

"That's one," Cyril said. "If you took some of the goulash from Gorvonia, don't eat it."

Dina gave an anguished cry. "Oh, no! My glorious goulash, spoiled? Where is that wretched Rethal? I'll take every last bite and stuff it down his throat!"

Nancy tugged at Cyril's sleeve. "The stuffed squash," she said in a stage whisper. "Vlad's dish."

"And skip the stuffed squash from Rethalstan, too," Cyril announced. "Did any of you notice anything else you had doubts about?"

There was an uneasy silence.

"The vegetable curry is pretty spicy," someone said in a hesitant voice.

"Curry is supposed to be spicy," someone else said.

"You want spicy, try the Jamaican jerk chicken," another guy contributed. "It'll put the top of your head into orbit!"

"Or the filé gumbo," Penny said, in an exaggerated Cajun accent. "I guar-on-tee it."

There was still an edge to the laughter, but Nancy could tell the moment of panic had passed.

"Ned?" she said in a low voice. "Do you know the guy who made the joke about stomach pumps? Somebody should ask him a few questions."

Ned shook his head. "I know him by sight, that's all. I'll see if I can find out his name." He stood up, and headed off to search.

Nancy turned to Bess and George. "Bess, will you go look around the kitchen area?" she asked. "The usual—anything that seems out of place. And, George, see if you can get Dina to calm down long enough to tell you all about her goulash. When and where she made it, where it was stored, whatever."

"You got it," George said. "What about you?"

"I'm going to try to get a list of helpers from Penny," Nancy replied. "Then we'll divide them up. There's always a chance that somebody saw something."

J. P. had been following the discussion. "Would you like me to talk to Vlad?" he asked. "His dish was ruined, too, after all. If nothing else, I can try to keep him and Dina from assaulting each other."

"Good idea," Nancy said. "Thanks."

Penny was standing behind the serving table as if frozen in place. She looked near tears. When Nancy approached, she blurted out, "There was nothing wrong before. I know that. I tasted Dina's dish yesterday, when she brought it over. It was delicious."

"That's important evidence," Nancy said. "You didn't try Vlad's squash, too, did you?"

"I wish I had," Penny replied. "It looks so inviting. What kind of creep would do such a thing? What if somebody got sick?"

"I guess whoever did it didn't care about that," Nancy said. "Tell me about this morning. You and

Lance brought the cartons over from Food Services. What then?"

Penny gave her a sidelong look. "You were there. We put everything in the fridge, remember? Then, about an hour ago, we went back and started heating the dishes that needed it."

" 'We,' " Nancy repeated. "You mean, you and Lance?"

"No, a couple of other girls and me," Penny replied. "Humera and Marie-Christine. That's Humera over there, by the shish-kebob. I don't see Marie-Christine just now."

Nancy glanced over. Humera was short with wavy black hair and dark eyes. She had a brightly patterned scarf tied around her hips, over a pair of white jeans.

"In between, while the food was in the fridge, was the kitchen kept locked?" Nancy asked.

Penny frowned in concentration. "Well . . . most of the time, sure. But I can't swear about all the time. When we were going in and out, we left it open."

"So there were times when it was open and no one was there?" Nancy pursued.

"I guess," Penny said reluctantly.

"One more thing," Nancy said. "If somebody wanted to ruin Dina's dish by pouring sugar in it, how easy would that be?"

Penny looked puzzled. "You lift the foil and pour it in, that's all. What do you mean?"

"I mean, how easy would it have been to *pick out* Dina's dish?" Nancy said.

"Oh. Got you," Penny said. "Hmm . . . Pretty easy, I guess. All the trays were labeled. We needed to tell which was which. And Dina's would have been especially easy. It was at the top of a stack."

"Really? How do you happen to remember that?" Nancy asked.

"When we got the cartons to the kitchen, I counted the dishes," Penny told her. "There were two missing. We had to go back for them."

"Oh, yes. I remember," Nancy said. "And Dina's was one of them?"

"That's right," Penny said. She narrowed her eyes. "That's funny—the other one was Vlad's."

Nancy asked more questions, but Penny didn't have anything to add. She did give Nancy the names of those helpers she recalled. It was a short list.

Nancy thanked her and went over to speak to Humera. She told pretty much the same story as Penny. She had not noticed anybody's doing anything out of the ordinary. She couldn't imagine why anybody would do anything so mean. Whoever did it should be forced to eat every bit of the spoiled dishes.

As Nancy left Humera, she saw Ned wave and beckon and she went to him.

"I found that guy," he reported. "His name's Clay.

He plays bass in a garage-rock group on campus called the Road Kills."

"Yuck," Nancy said, making a face. "Is their music as gross as their name?"

"Probably," Ned said with a grin. "Anyway, I think we can cross him off our list of suspects. He doesn't know anybody in the IFC and couldn't care less about the organization, the festival, or much of anything except his group and his attitude."

"Then why was he helping in the kitchen?" Nancy wondered.

Ned's grin widened. "He wasn't helping, just hanging out. There's this girl he's got his eye on . . ."

Nancy groaned. "I can fill in the rest. Okay, he's off the list."

George joined them. "Dina is steaming," she reported. "You can imagine. She swears the goulash was perfect when she gave it to Penny yesterday."

"Penny confirms that," Nancy interjected.

"Oh? Good," George said. "That's about it. The rest was all about sneaky Rethals. She's a thousand percent convinced Vlad poisoned her dish. I pointed out that his dish got ruined, too. She said that was a typical Rethal trick to throw off suspicion. I got really tired of listening to all that stuff. Why can't they work it out, instead of acting like a couple of cross four-year-olds?"

"She was brought up to hate those other people and blame them for whatever went wrong," Ned said. "The same with Vlad, on his side. It's hard to get away from something that's been with you so long."

"That's not all," Nancy said. "When Vlad says or does something Dina doesn't like, that just proves she's right about him and his people. And the way she reacts proves to him he's right to suspect her and her people."

"Life's a lot simpler when you're a detective," George said with a straight face. "You get to suspect *everyone,* regardless of race, creed, or national origin."

They all laughed.

Bess came rushing up. "Look!" she panted. "I just found this in the kitchen trash."

She held out a crumpled brown paper bag. Nancy took it and looked inside. She saw two plastic shakers, meant for picnics or for keeping on the table. One was labeled Salt, the other had held a powdered artificial sweetener. The tops were pried off both of them.

Ned peered over Nancy's shoulder. "Bess, you're fantastic," he enthused. "This could be the clue that cracks the case."

Bess turned pink with pleasure. "Wait, there's more," she said. "This was in the trash, too."

She produced a cash register receipt.

"This wasn't inside the bag?" Nancy asked.

Bess shook her head. "No. It was stuck to the bottom of it. But look, it's for just two items, and the prices match the ones on the two containers. That can't be a coincidence."

Nancy and Ned examined the receipt. "I know this place," Ned said. "It's a convenience store two or three blocks from campus."

"It's dated yesterday at two-sixteen P.M.," Nancy said. "Good work, Bess. This is the most solid fact we have so far."

"Now all we have to do is find out where everyone was at two-sixteen," George said. "Why don't we start with you, Ned?"

"Uh, sure," Ned said. He scratched the back of his head. "Let's see, two-sixteen . . . I must have been done with lunch, but it was a while before you guys showed up. . . . I know Cyril and I spent some time firming up plans for the weekend. Or was that in the morning, after class?"

He paused. His face reddened. "I guess I don't really know," he admitted. "Who keeps track of what he's doing every minute?"

Nancy grinned. "My dad, for one," she said. "He's a lawyer. His time is what he gets paid for."

"Still, there's a point," George said. "It's not necessarily suspicious if somebody can't account for his time."

"No," Nancy agreed. "But if somebody *can,* that's a point in his favor."

At Nancy's suggestion they fanned out in search of the leading IFC members. Twenty minutes later they met again in front of the IFC booth.

"Any alibis for yesterday at two-sixteen?" Nancy asked, looking around the little circle.

"Nope," Ned said. George shook her head.

Bess gave them a smug look. "I have one," she said. "Guess who? Vlad! He was playing tennis yesterday between two and three. I got the name of his partner, so we can check it out."

"If he told you who he was playing with, it's bound to check out," George said.

"A friend could have bought the stuff for him while he was playing tennis," Ned pointed out.

Nancy considered that. "True," she said. "But it's a pretty weird favor to ask somebody. What if the other guy hears about the sabotage at lunch today and starts wondering? Why take the risk?"

Bess suddenly grabbed Nancy's arm. "Oh, no!" she gasped. "I don't believe it."

"What is it?" Nancy asked in alarm.

"Dina just went into the tent backstage," Bess said breathlessly. "Do you know who was with her? Cheb Rachid, the lead singer of the Rai Rebels!"

"Oh, that's right," Nancy said. "I meant to tell you. I saw some of the group with her earlier. Do you want to meet them? Come on."

"I couldn't!" Bess exclaimed, pulling back.

"Of course you could," Nancy said with a laugh. As they neared the yellow-and-green tent, Dina came out. Her face was strained. When she saw them, she brightened.

"Do you think it would be okay to say hi to the Rai Rebels?" Nancy asked her. "Bess is a big fan."

"I am sure they would love it," Dina replied. "They are far from home, and not so many people here have heard of them yet."

The tent had an old-fashioned look. Nancy wondered if Emerson College had bought it years earlier from a circus that went out of business. She pulled the flap of the door aside and pushed Bess through. The light inside was subdued, filtered through the colored canvas. Half a dozen folding chairs were scattered near the central pole.

The musicians were standing around a table that held a platter of sandwiches, a bowl of fruit, and bottles of water and soda. Most of them wore gold or red satin shirts with billowy sleeves and flowing collars. One, with thick, curly hair and a cute smile, wore black jeans and a black shirt with the top buttons undone and the tails hanging out.

"That's Rachid," Bess whispered.

Rachid spotted them and came over. "Hello," he said. "Is it already the hour?"

It took Nancy a moment to realize he was asking if it was time for the group to go on. She glanced at Bess, who looked tongue-tied.

"No, no," Nancy said. "We just wanted to meet you and say how much we like your music."

"Thank you very much," Rachid said. His teeth gleamed when he smiled. "It is an honor to be here."

Nancy wondered if standing right next to a star was making her dizzy. Then she realized that it wasn't her. She was still standing straight up. But the heavy wooden pole that supported the tent wasn't. It was tilting to the right, ever so slowly at first, then with increasing speed.

The tent was collapsing—and they were trapped under it!

8

In-Tents Danger

"Look out," Nancy shouted. "Everybody down!"

The members of the band looked around, startled. Rachid snapped a warning in Arabic.

Nancy did not wait to see how they reacted. She grabbed one of the metal chairs and put it on top of another. Then she did the same again with another pair of chairs.

By now the heavy, dusty canvas was billowing down around them. Nancy fell to her knees and ducked between the two sets of chairs. Bess and Rachid crawled in next to her. The chairs kept the canvas a few inches above their heads.

With a loud crack the tent pole hit the table. The

platter of fruit shattered. An apple bounced to the ground and rolled into Nancy's knee.

The edge of the table bent, but the table was strong enough to support the fallen tent pole.

Nancy sneezed once from the dust, then called out, "Are you all right? Is anybody hurt?"

A voice replied, "Okay here."

"Let's get out of here," Bess pleaded.

"Good idea," Nancy said. "Which way *is* out?"

As if by magic, the tent pole started to rise again. Nancy realized that people on the outside must be pulling at the guy ropes. Daylight streamed in as somebody tugged open the flaps at the entrance. "Over here," an anxious voice called.

"We're coming," Nancy called back. By now there was enough room to stand up, so long as she stooped. She helped Bess to her feet, then said to Rachid, "This way."

The members of the Rai Rebels followed Nancy and Bess outside to freedom. She noticed that each of the musicians was carrying his instrument. Good thinking. If the tent could fall down once, it might fall down again. But exactly *why* had it collapsed like that? An accident? Or something more sinister?

The fall of the tent had attracted a crowd. Dina and Cyril were trying to move people back. Ned and George pushed through to Nancy's side.

"Are you okay?" Ned demanded. "What happened?"

"I'm fine, and I don't know what happened," Nancy replied. "Not yet."

She looked around. At the back, two men in Emerson College coveralls were holding the corners of the tent while a third man fastened the guy ropes to metal stakes. Nancy went over to him. She noticed *Mike* stitched in red over the pocket of his coverall. He glanced up as Nancy approached.

"Can I help you?" he asked. His tone said, Go away and don't bother me.

"I was inside the tent just now," Nancy said. "Why did it fall down? Were the ropes loose?"

"No way," Mike said emphatically. "Some joker untied them, that's what. And if I find out who . . ."

"You're sure?" Nancy asked. Mike scowled and nodded sharply. "How hard would it be to do that? Would it take long?"

"Easy as kiss my hand," Mike replied. "Look—this here's called a clove hitch. Great knot, holds like iron. But say you want to undo it. All you do is give yourself a little slack and—"

With a deft gesture, he unfastened the rope. Then, just as quickly, he retied it to the stake. "Anything else?" he asked.

"No," Nancy said. "Thanks for your help."

Mike unbent enough to mumble, "You're welcome."

Nancy told Ned, George, and Bess what she'd

learned. "Let's see if anybody noticed someone at the back of the tent," she suggested.

They moved through the crowd asking questions. The answers were discouraging. No one had seen anyone behind the tent, or if he had, had not paid attention and couldn't describe the person.

The sound system suddenly crackled to life. Cyril's voice said, "Here's something to whet your appetite for tonight's dance and tomorrow's giant concert. It's a great honor for me to introduce a super group that comes to us all the way from Oran, Algeria. Let's give a real Emerson College welcome to . . . *the Rai Rebels!*"

The crowd cheered as the members of the group dashed onstage and took their places. Rachid was the last. He grabbed the mike and shouted, "Thank you! *Merci beaucoup!*" Over a sequence of minor chords from the keyboard, the lead guitarist laid down a hypnotic riff that was echoed by the syncopated beat of the drums.

Even before Rachid started singing, the audience was on its feet, swaying from side to side, hands waving in the air. From where Nancy was standing at the back, the audience looked like a wheat field swept by a breeze.

Bess grabbed Nancy's left hand and raised it. Nancy smiled and reached out with her right hand to Ned. He in turn linked hands with George. Together they swayed to the insistent beat of the music.

For those few moments Nancy let herself be carried away. But the moment the song ended, she went back to the question that kept circling in her head. Who was trying to trash the Worldbeat Festival, and just as puzzling, why?

Vlad and Dina were each convinced the other was doing it because of the election campaign. But what sense did that make? Suppose the motive was to make the other guy look bad and lose the election. What if it worked? If the sabotage campaign made the festival fail, it would have a terrible effect on the IFC. What was the point of plotting to wreck the organization you wanted to head up?

There was another possiblity that gave Nancy a chill. The bad feelings between Vlad and Dina, and between their countries, ran deep. What if one of them simply didn't care who got hurt, as long as the other suffered?

After two more numbers, the Rai Rebels left the stage to a storm of applause. Cyril bounded up to the mike and reminded everyone that the group would play at the dance that evening and the concert the next afternoon. Then he introduced the Flynn Family, an Irish group of four musicians and three stepdancers.

"How can the IFC afford to have these groups come from all over the world?" Nancy asked Ned.

Ned smiled. "Most of them don't," he said. "Take the Flynns, for example. They're from somewhere near Chicago."

George overheard. "You mean they're not Irish after all?"

"Oh, sure they are," Ned replied. "Their parents are, anyway. And the girl playing pennywhistle won an All-Ireland championship a couple of years ago. But they grew up here in the States. Same with the ska group in tomorrow's concert. They're all Jamaicans, but they live in Brooklyn. One of our members who's from the islands put us in touch with them."

"What about the Rai Rebels, though?" Bess asked anxiously. "They really are from North Africa, aren't they?"

Ned nodded. "You bet. But we didn't have to pay their way here. We couldn't have afforded that. What happened was, another of our members is a big rai fan. He heard they were planning a trip to the States. So we found out who their agent was and managed to book them for this weekend."

"I'm so glad," Bess said. "That was just a little taste. I can't wait to see them again. Nancy, can you take a minute to come look at Joann's booth? It's really worth it."

"I'd love to," Nancy replied. She followed Bess through the crowd to the bazaar area. It was clearly a hit with Emerson students. Every booth had people browsing through whatever it offered: CDs, clothing, and posters seemed especially popular. The most crowded was a booth selling African drums and percussion instruments. Nancy was tempted to pause to try a talking drum, but Bess kept walking.

"That's Joann's booth," Bess said, pointing. "But I don't see her. I wonder where she is?"

Joann had hung lengths of batik fabric along the back and sides of the booth. Displayed on a cloth-draped table at the rear of the space were fifteen or twenty delicately carved animals in a soft-looking wood. They ranged in size from an elephant no bigger than an egg to a cranelike bird that stood two feet high.

A blond girl wearing an embroidered dress and a head scarf came over to them. "Hello," she said. "You're visitors of Ned Nickerson, aren't you?"

"That's right," Nancy said. She introduced Bess and herself.

"I am Alina Orsulak," the girl said. "I am watching the booth for Joann. The animals are beautiful, are they not? And very popular. In just one hour I have sold five. One was my favorite, a mischievous-looking orangutan."

"I'm sorry we missed seeing it," Nancy said. "I'd love to know more about these figures. Are they all real animals, or are some of them imaginary?"

Alina laughed. "I know very little," she admitted. "But Joann will return very soon. She was expecting delivery of a package with more animals. Who knows? Maybe there will be another orangutan. If so, I think I will buy it myself."

Nancy and Bess were taking a closer look at the sculptures when Ned and George arrived.

Ned waved to Alina and turned to Nancy and Bess.

77

"Cyril's called an emergency meeting of the IFC steering committee," he announced. "He'd like you guys to be there, too, if you don't mind."

"Sure," Nancy said. "When and where?"

"In five minutes, inside the gym," Ned replied. "Alina, when will Joann be back? She should come to the meeting if she can."

"Very soon," Alina said again. "I will tell her. I can stay here longer if she needs me to."

"Thanks," Ned said. "You're a big help."

Nancy and her friends followed Ned out through the balloon-arch entrance to the bazaar and down a path to the front door of the gymnasium. Inside was an anteroom lined with trophy cases. Above the cases, framed photos of sports teams and individual athletes covered the walls.

Cyril, Penny, J. P., and Lance were seated around one half of a big round table. Dina was alone across from them. For a moment Nancy was reminded of a prisoner facing a panel of judges. Then she noticed Dina's expression. She decided it was more likely Dina was judging the others, and not very favorably.

Vlad was to one side, leaning against one of the display cases with his hands in his pockets. Akai, next to him, was reading the plaques on the trophies. A couple of other people, whom Nancy hadn't yet met, were also standing.

"Pull up a pew," Cyril said to Nancy and her friends. He waved to the empty chairs and waited for them to sit down. "I called this meeting because I am very concerned. In my view, the very existence of the IFC is under attack."

"Isn't that a little exaggerated?" Lance said. "A couple of practical jokes—"

Dina interrupted him. "You call it a practical joke to ruin my goulash?"

"And my stuffed squash?" Vlad demanded.

"And the whole buffet lunch I worked so hard to put together?" Penny cried. "How could you!"

"Hey, all I meant is no one got hurt," Lance said, retreating. "I didn't say it was funny."

"They could have been," Cyril pointed out. "Someone could have had a bad allergic reaction. Someone could have been hit by that falling tent pole, too. And who can guess what the next so-called joke might be? I don't know the legalities here, but if someone *is* hurt, we are responsible morally. We invited people to this event, after all. We have an obligation to keep it safe for them."

"So what can we do?" J. P. wondered. "Call off the festival? It's a little late for that. We're already in the middle of it."

"I know," Cyril replied. He paused to nod to Joann, who slipped into a chair. "But it seems to me the root of the problem isn't the festival, it's the IFC election. I'm not accusing anyone, but we all know how much tension and hostility have developed around it."

"We know who is to blame, too," Vlad growled.

"We certainly do," Dina shot back.

"That sort of exchange is exactly what I'm talking about," Cyril said. "It's dividing the club and poisoning people's relationships. That is why I've decided to ask both you, Dina, and you, Vlad, to withdraw your names from contention. You are both valuable members of the organization, and either of you might make a good president. With things as they are, though, it will be a disaster whichever of you is elected. What do you say?"

"If they withdraw, what then?" J. P. asked. "No one else is running."

"As president, I have the authority to postpone the election," Cyril said. "We can put it off until we have someone to stand who's widely acceptable."

"Aha!" Vlad said, straightening up. "I see now. This is nothing but an underhanded scheme to keep a Rethal from gaining high office."

"That's not so," Cyril said. "I—"

Vlad's voice rose to a shout. "I warn you, Cyril. I warn all of you. We are a proud people. We know very well how to deal with insults! You will see, and you will be very sorry!"

He stomped over to the door, slammed it open, and stormed out.

9

Walkout After Walkout

Vlad's dramatic exit was followed by a long silence. The crash of the door still seemed to echo in the room.

Cyril gave a sigh. "I *am* sorry he took it that way," he said. "I suppose I might have expected it."

Dina stood up abruptly. "How else could he take it?" she demanded. "When faced with a coup d'etat, resistance is the only principled course."

Nancy stared at Dina, then exchanged glances with George and Bess. They looked as baffled as she was. What was Dina talking about?

"A coup d'etat?" Ned said. "Come on, Dina. Get serious. Cyril doesn't *want* to stay president. He simply thinks we need time to cool off."

Dina sniffed. "You Americans!" she said, with a mixture of affection and contempt. "In so many ways you are such amazing people. But where politics is concerned, you are like little children. A series of strange events takes place. With that as an excuse, an official cancels an election. He tries to bully into silence those who would succeed him. What is the result? He stays in power. Now ask yourself. To whose benefit were those strange events?"

Penny stared at her. "Dina, do you really think *Cyril*—"

"I accuse no one," Dina said, breaking in. "But a Gorvonian is never intimidated by unfair tactics. I am still a candidate for president of the IFC. I intend to win. And I warn you, if the election does not take place as announced, I will go to the college officials. I will demand that the IFC be dissolved!"

Everyone in the room started talking at once. Dina swept the table with a cold glance. Then, like Vlad, she stalked out. Unlike Vlad, she did not slam the door.

Cyril rapped his knuckles on the table. "May we please have some order?"

"Shhh!" Penny said. "Come on, people!"

Slowly quiet returned.

"I have a statement to make," Cyril announced. "We in the IFC have taken on an important mission here at Emerson. We want to promote international friendship and understanding. And I believe we do a pretty fair job of carrying out that mission."

"Hear, hear!" J. P. murmured.

Cyril gave him a grateful glance, then continued. "I've liked serving as president. I was looking forward to passing the job on. However, I will not let all we've worked so hard to build be destroyed by factionalism. Unless I see some radical improvement in the climate inside the club, I intend to stand for reelection. If that happens, my platform will be to build unity and to combat any effort to bring external quarrels into the IFC."

"Hear, hear!" J. P. said again. Some of the others clapped.

Nancy was not happy about the direction her thoughts were taking. Only moments before, Dina had accused Cyril of plotting to hold onto the presidency of the IFC. Now he was announcing a plan to run for reelection. That gave Dina's accusations more weight.

Nancy realized that she didn't know Cyril at all. He seemed nice enough on first acquaintance. Bess had certainly taken to him, and not just because of his cute accent. The fact that he and Ned were friends was another big point in his favor. But was he the kind of sneak who would sabotage an important event for the sake of political advantage? She did not want to think so, but she had to admit she didn't know.

She would have to ask Ned . . . but very, very carefully. She and Ned had a great relationship. They could tell each other anything. Still, she wasn't sure how he would react if he found out she suspected his friend. At the very least, it might put a cloud over what she wanted to be a super weekend.

"Cyril, what can we do?" Joann asked. She sounded very distressed. "The festival means so much. We can't let anyone ruin it."

"I'm with you on that," Cyril replied. "But we have a secret weapon. You may not know it, but our guests, Nancy, Bess, and George, are super detectives. When it comes to solving mysteries and foiling evil plots, there's no one to touch them."

Everyone turned to look at them. Nancy felt her cheeks grow warm. Ned patted her shoulder.

"That's wonderful!" Penny exclaimed. "I move we appoint Nancy Drew and her friends official IFC investigators."

"I second the motion," J. P. said. He caught George's eye and smiled.

"All in favor?" Cyril looked around the room. "The motion passes. But we didn't ask if they're willing to serve."

"We'll be glad to help if we can," Nancy said.

"Good for you, mate," Cyril said. "You let us know what we can do."

When the meeting broke up, Nancy, Ned, George, and Bess held a strategy meeting outside across from the gym.

"We've got two jobs to do," Nancy said. "We have to find out who's in back of these tricks. We also have to keep the festival from being spoiled."

"Make that three," Ned said. "If we don't solve this, the IFC may go down in flames."

"It may anyway," George said. "I haven't been seeing a lot of international friendship lately."

"That's not fair," Bess asserted. "Most of the kids in the club are really nice. They'd get along fine if it weren't for all this tension."

The discussion was drifting away from the point. Nancy pulled it back. "What are we looking at?" she said, jotting some notes on an index card. "Dina got hit with that e-mail yesterday, and the drawing on her door. Then a threatening call last night. This morning someone switched Vlad's videotape."

"Putting stuff in the food at lunch," George added.

"And that tent falling on us," Bess said with a shudder.

"I don't get it," Ned said, rubbing his chin. "Who's the target here? Dina? Vlad? And neither of them was inside the tent when it fell down."

"How about this?" George suggested. "Vlad sent the e-mail and made the drawing and the crank call. Dina figured he was the one, so to get back at him she switched the videotape."

"And who monkeyed with the food?" Bess asked. "Both of their dishes were ruined."

"I don't know," George said. She sounded frustrated. "Whoever did it must have doctored both dishes to throw off suspicion."

"Well, it sure worked on me," Bess retorted. "I thought both of them looked really mad."

Nancy studied her notes. "Vlad has an alibi for the time when the salt and sweetener were bought," she pointed out. "And Dina couldn't have made the crank call. I was right there in the room with her when it came through."

"A tape recorder and an auto dialer," Ned said.

Nancy wrinkled her nose at him. "I thought of that, smarty," she said. "But when Dina asked who it was, he answered. Okay, maybe you could rig some gadget to do that, but let's be real. Would a college student have access to such complicated gear? I don't think so. Besides, why bother?"

"That's the big question," George said. "Why would anybody go to so much trouble to win an election in a campus club? I can't help feeling there's more to this than we've seen so far."

"I know what you mean," Nancy said somberly. "We'd better keep a very sharp eye out."

"Is this straight?" Ned called from the top of a tall ladder.

Nancy backed away and looked carefully at the flag Ned was fastening to the wall. "The left corner's a little low," she reported. "Okay, that's good."

Ned put a length of doublefaced tape behind the cloth and pressed. He waited to make sure it held, then clambered down the ladder. "Whew," he said, looking around the gym. "Funny—thirty flags didn't sound like many when Cyril asked me to put them up."

"They're very attractive," Bess said. "All those different colors."

"It's great, like a World Cup final," George observed.

A bunch of IFC members were decorating the gym for that night's dance. The maintenance people had already set up tables and chairs around the perimeter. Up on stage, three roadies in jeans and tank tops checked the wiring on the sound equipment.

"I could do with some supper," Cyril announced when they had all finished their jobs. "What do you say to Mama Maria's?"

"That's an Italian place a couple of blocks away," Ned explained to Nancy. "I love the lasagna. The prices are reasonable, too."

"I can't," Joann told Cyril. She sounded depressed. "I need to rest before the dance."

"I can't, either," Penny said cheerfully. "Lance is taking me to Le Perigord Vert for dinner."

"Ooh la la!" Cyril cracked. "That's that posh place in the mansion by the lake, isn't it?"

"That's right," Penny said. "The cuisine is supposed to be really special. I can't wait."

"What's the occasion?" Bess asked. "Your birthday?"

Penny laughed. "No, nothing like that. Lance loves

gourmet cooking. Since he inherited some money from his uncle, we've been trying out all the fine restaurants around here."

"Pretty tough work," George observed. "But I guess somebody's got to do it."

Penny went off to change for her dinner date. Joann went off to rest. Everyone else walked over to Mama Maria's and took a big table in the back. Nancy liked the antipasto and the lasagna. She enjoyed the company and the easy conversation, too. Even so, she couldn't shake the feeling that this was the calm before the storm. She was sure of it. Her only question was, what form would the storm take?

Eager students started lining up outside the gym half an hour before the dance was scheduled to begin. Cyril and the others took care of last-minute chores. Nancy, George, and Bess walked around searching for anything that seemed out of the ordinary—they didn't find a thing.

Lance rushed in just before the doors were supposed to open. His white shirt, striped tie, and sport coat made him look as if he were coming from a job interview. Nancy helped him move a table in front of the inner doors. He set the cash box and a roll of numbered tickets on the table, put a brown manila envelope on the seat of his chair, and took a rubber stamp and ink pad from his jacket pocket.

"For stamping people's hands after they pay?" Nancy asked. "You came prepared."

"It's the only way," Lance replied.

J. P. was standing by the outer doors. He gave Lance a questioning look.

"Let 'er rip!" Lance called.

J. P. opened the doors. The excited crowd flowed in and lined up at the table. Nancy got out of the way.

Inside, the music had already started. The plan was to switch on and off between live groups and recorded sounds. A Somali student was serving as deejay. His taste roamed the globe, from Argentinian tangos and Nigerian highlife to French rap, Russian techno, and Japanese funk. Fortunately, he announced each number before he played it. Otherwise, Nancy knew she would never have been sure what she was listening to.

"Did you see?" Bess asked Nancy and Ned, during a lull while a samba band set up. "Vlad's here. Not only that, I saw him dancing."

"I saw Dina, too," Ned reported. "She was helping Lance out front. I'm glad. Maybe both of them have had second thoughts."

"Maybe," George said in a skeptical tone. "Or maybe it hit them that they wouldn't get many votes if they *didn't* show up tonight."

The Rai Rebels, when they appeared, went over really well with the crowd. Later, a Cajun band had everyone on the floor trying to learn the two-step.

"Whew!" Nancy panted, after a wild uptempo number. "This is harder than a session at the gym!"

"It *is* a session at the gym," Ned pointed out with a grin.

Nancy was working on a retort when Cyril hurried over to them. His face was white.

"We have a problem," he said in a low voice.

Nancy and Ned followed him to a quiet corner.

"What's the matter?" Nancy asked.

"Lance just looked inside the envelope where he was keeping the proceeds," Cyril replied. "There was nothing there but cut-up paper. No money. Several thousand dollars in untraceable cash, all gone!"

10

Paper Chase

Nancy and Ned quickly followed Cyril across the dance floor. Along the way as Nancy spotted George and Bess, she motioned them to come along. Cyril led them through a side door into a corridor lined with offices.

Lance was waiting in a classroom. His face was pale and there were beads of sweat along his hairline. His maroon polo shirt showed damp splotches. Penny, next to him, had tear stains on her cheeks.

"I swear, Cyril," Lance burst out, when he saw them come through the doorway. "I have no idea how—"

Cyril held up a hand, palm outward, like a traffic cop stopping a car. "Easy, mate. No cause to fret. We'll soon sort it all out."

On a table near Lance, Nancy noticed a metal cash box and a bulging manila envelope with the flap undone. A few pieces of typing paper, cut roughly to the size of a dollar bill, had escaped from the envelope and lay scattered across the tabletop.

"Nancy," Cyril said. "You're our official investigator. What do we do now?"

"From what you told me, this is a case of grand larceny," Nancy replied. "That's a serious felony. We'd better call the police, right away."

"The police!" Penny gasped. "Oh, no! We can't!"

"Why not?" Bess asked her.

"Well . . ." Penny began. She seemed to grope for words. "Our members. Lots of them are from countries where the police are . . . well, where most people don't trust them. If they think we're connected to the police, they may drop out of the IFC. Besides, once the police are on it, everything will have to come out. There'll be a huge scandal. It'll wreck the festival."

"And cops don't understand what campus life is like," Lance said. "Who knows what they'd make of the fight between Vlad and Dina, for instance."

Cyril frowned. "We can't cover up a major theft," he said slowly. "I imagine that would be a crime itself. But suppose we went to the police with the crime already solved. They wouldn't need to poke into things as much, would they? It'd be better all around."

"I think I catch your drift," Ned said. He gave Nancy a sympathetic look.

"So do I," Nancy said. "All right, we'll see what we can do. But we can't hold off reporting this for long. Unless we can unmask the thief by the end of the festival tomorrow afternoon, we'll have to bring in the police. And believe me, they won't be happy with us for delaying."

Cyril's shoulders slumped forward a little in relief. "Thanks," he said. "I know this isn't the sort of weekend you were expecting, Nancy. Sorry we couldn't oblige."

"It's certainly turning out to be interesting," Nancy told him. She turned to Lance. "That's the envelope the money was in?"

"That's right," Lance replied. "At least, it looks the same."

"What happened?"

"I wish I knew," Lance said. He shook his head. "I was taking admissions the same way I usually do. I made change from the cash box and put the bigger bills away as they came in."

"You put them in the envelope, you mean," George said. "I noticed you do that earlier, at the picnic."

"That's right," Lance said.

"Where did you keep the envelope?" Bess wondered.

"I put a chair behind the table next to me," Lance explained. "The envelope was on the seat of the chair. I know it sounds pretty careless, after what happened.

All I can say is, it made sense at the time. I never let it out of my sight. That's what's so weird."

"You were at the admissions table the whole time, nonstop?" Nancy asked.

"Well, no, I did take a break partway through," Lance admitted. "Joann covered for me. I wasn't gone long."

"Did you look inside the envelope when you got back?" George asked.

The question seemed to surprise Lance. He thought for a moment, then said, "Not exactly. But I'm pretty sure I put more bills in it after that. I think I would have noticed if anything was wrong."

Nancy turned to Bess and George. "Would one of you see if you can find Joann?" she asked.

"She went back to the dorm," Penny said. "She's been feeling pretty low. I think seeing all these kids having fun just made it worse."

"I'll go," George volunteered. She left.

"So how long did you stay at the table, and when did you discover the money was missing?" Nancy asked.

"I closed up shop about an hour ago," Lance said. "I figured anybody who'd already missed most of the dance ought to get in free. Besides, I'd promised Penny I wouldn't stay on duty the whole time. What's the point of a dance if you don't dance?"

"What did you do with the envelope and cash box, then?" Ned asked. "You didn't carry it around on the dance floor."

Lance looked abashed. "No, I went downstairs and put it in my locker. It was perfectly safe. It has a top-notch combination lock on it. And when Cyril and I went down to get the stuff, it hadn't been disturbed. We brought everything up here to count the proceeds. Then we opened the envelope and saw it was stuffed with paper. What a mess!"

Nancy rubbed her forehead. It helped her concentrate. "So you were behind the table, with the envelope in plain sight, the whole time—"

"Except when Joann took over," Lance interjected.

"Right," Nancy said. "Then you carried the envelope straight to your locker and locked it inside. But when you and Cyril retrieved it, the money had vanished."

"I know it sounds impossible," Lance said desperately. "But that's what happened."

"You're right, it sounds impossible," Ned said. "Lance, are you one hundred percent sure that you were right there behind the table every minute of the time? Except for Joann, I mean."

"Of course I'm—" Lance's face changed. "Hold on! I just remembered. There were these two clowns who started getting into a fight. I went over to cool them down. They called me a name and left. But I wasn't away from the table for more than a minute or two."

"That's all it would have taken," Nancy said. "Did you recognize the guys? Would you know them again?"

Lance shook his head. "Nope. Sorry. They were just two guys. You mean it was all staged?"

"It sounds that way," Nancy replied. "They distracted you and drew you away from the table long enough for their accomplice to grab the money. It's my guess that they came prepared with an envelope and simply switched it for yours. Anybody who had watched you collecting money at lunch would know you kept the big bills in a manila envelope."

"Boy, what a sap I am," Lance said bitterly.

There was a silence. Apparently no one felt like arguing the point.

After a few moments Penny said, "That's just a theory, though, isn't it? I mean, no one saw it happen that way."

"No," Nancy agreed. "But it does fit the facts pretty well. Another question, Lance. Can you tell if this is your envelope, or a substitute?"

Lance reached for the envelope.

"Hold on!" Ned exclaimed. "Don't touch it!"

"What do you mean, touch it? I already carried it around and then opened it," Lance protested.

"Ned's right, Lance," Nancy said. "We shouldn't handle it any more than we have to. It's crucial evidence. Sure, every crook alive knows about fingerprints, but they slip up all the same."

Nancy glanced around the room. There was a plastic bag lining the trash basket near the door. She went over and checked it out. It was empty, so she took it out.

"We can keep the envelope in this to protect it," she announced. "Lance, do you see anything different about it?"

Lance frowned. "It's just a nine-by-twelve manila envelope," he said. "They all look the same. I guess this isn't as crumpled as I remember, but it's nothing I could swear to."

With Ned's help, Nancy used a pencil to push the envelope and its contents into the plastic bag. Just as they finished, the door of the room was flung open. Dina ran into the small room. Her face was flushed and her eyes were wide.

"What is this I hear!" she shouted.

George and Joann came in behind her. "Sorry," George said apologetically. She eased the door closed. "We ran into Dina. She knew something was up and asked me what it was. I thought she ought to know. I didn't think she'd go off like a Roman candle."

"It's okay, George," Nancy said. "We ought to get Vlad in here, too."

It was as if the sound of his name was a summoning spell. The door banged open again, and in came Vlad and J. P.

"So!" Vlad hissed. "Secret conferences—a conspiracy! I see it now!"

"Oh, do come in and be quiet," Cyril said. "Stop sounding like a spy in a silly cartoon."

For a moment Vlad's face seemed to swell like a balloon about to pop. He breathed loudly and heavily a few times, then moved to the sidelines.

"Now, here's the situation," Cyril began. He quickly summarized the theft of the envelope. "Nancy? Over to you."

"Joann," Nancy said. "When you stood in for Lance, was there a lot of money in the brown envelope?"

"So I thought," Joann responded. "I do not know. It did not seem right to leave such valuables on a chair. I put it on the table and put the cash box on top of it."

"You didn't look inside?" Bess asked.

"Oh, no, there was no reason," Joann told her. "When Lance returned and Dina came over, he put the envelope back on the chair. I do not think he looked inside, either."

"Lance?" Nancy queried.

"Um, yes, that's right," Lance said. "I'd forgotten that. After Joann left, I was busy briefing Dina. She helped me for a while."

"Helped you collect money, you mean?" George asked.

Dina spoke up. "I gave tickets and stamped hands," she said. "Lance dealt with money."

"That's right," Lance confirmed.

"I smell a plot!" Vlad announced in a ringing voice.

"You smell, period!" Dina retorted.

"Why were you behind the table, just before so

much money disappeared?" Vlad demanded. He wagged an accusing finger in Dina's face.

Dina looked seriously tempted to bite his finger. Instead, she said, "Only one with a mind as low as the one that wrote that e-mail would even ask such a question. You are convicted out of your own mouth!"

"Take it easy, you two," J. P. called. They ignored him.

"I wrote no e-mail against you," Vlad said in an icy tone. "But I begin to believe the accusations it made. It would be terrible if money collected by the International Friendship Club went instead to those who preach hatred and violence."

"Your Rethal friends, you mean?" Dina replied, raising her voice.

Nancy saw major trouble brewing. She put a hand on Dina's shoulder. Dina shook it off without looking. At the same time Ned stepped up next to Vlad, ready to intervene if he had to.

"As a loyal Rethal, I am proud to have many Rethal friends," Vlad stated, staring past Ned's shoulder. "They do not need stolen money to spread their views. All true Rethals agree with them already. It is only those who wish to poison minds who will do anything to reach their goals."

"We have only one goal!" Dina shouted. "A united Gorvonia, free of all foreign oppressors!"

Vlad slowly shook his head. "I pity you, Dina," he said. "Your intelligence has not saved you from being duped. Those who control you do not want your loyalty. They want only what they can get from you—such as the money that belongs to the IFC."

"Lies! Slanders!" Dina shouted. "Shut your mouth, or I'll shut it for you!"

Fists clenched, she flung herself at Vlad.

11

A Mountain of Charges

The instant Nancy saw Dina start to move, she grabbed her shoulders. In that same moment Ned jumped in front of Vlad and clasped Dina's wrists.

"Hey, come on. Take it easy," Ned said.

Dina struggled to free her arms. Ned was unmoved.

"Please, Dina," Nancy said softly in her ear. "Acting like this will only hurt your cause."

Nancy stared past Dina and Ned at Vlad, who was standing very still, as if waiting for Dina's blows. His face was blank. Only his eyes moved.

Cyril and J. P. joined Ned. The three guys were like a wall blocking Dina's route to Vlad.

"We all need to cool off," Cyril said. "All the excitement today has us rattled."

Dina took a deep breath. In a voice that was almost normal, she said, "You heard him. You all heard him. He called me a thief and a swindler. He said I have robbed the IFC."

"When people get angry, they say things they don't mean," J. P. told her.

"Yes," Dina retorted. "And some people pretend to get angry so they can say things they know are lies!"

Bess muttered, "Puh-leese, don't start up again!"

"My honor has been dirtied!" Dina proclaimed.

"That is like saying the lake has been wettened," Vlad remarked.

He said it in an undertone, but loud enough for Dina to hear. Her face reddened and the cords of her neck stood out. Nancy was afraid she would try to attack Vlad again. Instead, she turned to Cyril.

"I demand that you and the steering committee of the IFC examine the club accounts at once," she said coldly. "I resign as treasurer, of course. I will not serve under a cloud of suspicion."

"No need of that," Cyril said quickly. "As for looking over the books, surely that can wait till morning. At this time of night, and after the day we've had, I'm not sure I could tell one number from another, much less add them."

"Even if the accounts are perfect, there is still the stolen money from tonight," Vlad pointed out. "You were at the admission table."

"How do we know you were not the one who took the money, while your henchmen distracted Lance?" Dina retorted.

Bess looked over at Nancy and rolled her eyes. They pressed their lips together to keep from infecting each other with giggles. Not that the theft of so much money was funny. Not at all. But Cyril was right. Vlad and Dina were acting like villains from a Saturday morning 'toon. All they needed to make the picture complete were swirly black capes and fake mustaches.

J. P. stepped forward. He scowled at Vlad and Dina. "You are both acting irresponsibly," he scolded. "Leave your private quarrels out of this. The club has lost a lot of money. We may lose our good name as well. This is a time to pull together, not fight among ourselves."

"Hear, hear!" Cyril said. He checked his watch. "It's late. Let's break up and give our official detectives some room to do their job. I'm calling a steering committee meeting for tomorrow morning at ten-thirty. We have a lot of issues to deal with."

Nancy heard groans from around the room, but no one disagreed with Cyril's decision.

The dance had ended. The gym was dark. Nancy and her friends paused outside as the others took off.

"Is anybody else hungry?" Bess asked.

"I could use a snack," George admitted.

"There's the all-night diner over on Grove Street," Ned said. "It's just a five-minute walk."

"Maybe it's just as well the others didn't come," Nancy said. "We need to talk."

They crossed the campus. Nancy was struck by how peaceful it seemed. From the window of a dorm room came the muted notes of a jazz tune. The only other sounds were the rustling of tree branches and the remote hum of a passing airliner.

Even at such a late hour the diner was half full. Ned waved to a couple of people as they walked to an empty booth in the far corner. The waitress brought them water and took their orders—a burger for Ned, a salad for George, and apple pie for Bess.

When it was Nancy's turn, she shook her head. "Just a glass of iced tea, please," she said.

"Okay," Ned said, when the waitress left. "First question: Is tonight's theft connected to the other incidents we've been dealing with?"

"I don't see why it should be," Bess said. "Sabotage is one thing, stealing's another. Different motives, different methods . . ."

"Isn't it an awfully big coincidence, having two sets of bad guys operating at the same time?" George asked dubiously.

"Not necessarily," Ned said. "The thieves may have figured we'd think that way."

Nancy dipped her index finger in the condensation from her water glass and drew circles on the tabletop. "Are we assuming that the money was stolen during that fight Lance told us about?"

"Well, of course," George said. "It's like, you're walking down the street and somebody with a hot dog gets ketchup on you. And while he helps you wipe it off, his partner steals your wallet."

"Or that other one I heard about," Ned said. "You go to catch a plane. At the security barrier you put the bag with your computer on the conveyor belt for the scanner. Somebody pushes ahead of you. When he goes through the gate, it buzzes. He empties his pockets and tries again. No good. He takes off his belt and his watch. Still no good. Finally he gives up and walks away. But by then his accomplice and your computer are halfway to Dallas."

"Before, we were looking for somebody inside the IFC," Nancy pointed out. "But Lance didn't recognize the guys who got into the fight."

"Say this is political," George suggested. "Whoever's in back of it would probably have friends off campus with the same beliefs who would be willing to help. They wouldn't even have to know the reason, just that it was to help the cause."

"So any two guys from—call it Country X—could be suspects," Ned said. "Whew. What a mess."

"Most people aren't going to take that kind of risk,"

Bess said. "Not unless they're desperate. If you just want to help some political cause, why not hold a bake sale instead?"

Nancy and the others laughed.

"Sure. I can see it now," Ned said. " 'Support extremism, buy a brownie!' "

"It *is* funny," Nancy said. "But Bess has a good point. Whoever did this must have a solid motive, not just the opportunity."

"I hate to say this," Bess said hesitantly. "But we know one person who needs money really badly, right away. If Joann can't pay her college bills, it could end up ruining her whole life."

Nancy nodded slowly. "I thought of that. And she was alone at the table when she relieved Lance. She could have easily switched the envelopes."

"Now, wait a minute," George protested. "I've gotten to know Joann a little. We talked a long time last night. Sure, she's very upset about her situation, even desperate. But she is not a crook!"

"What if she saw all that cash sitting there and she just couldn't stop herself?" Bess offered.

"I'm sorry, but that won't work," Nancy said. "If the envelope of cash had simply disappeared, maybe. But this was no spur of the moment crime. The thief had to have planned it. It took time to cut up the paper for the substitute envelope."

Their orders came. They put the conversation on

hold while they ate. Nancy accepted a few of Ned's french fries and a taste of Bess's pie, but it was just to be sociable. Her appetite was gone. She had a terrible feeling that, however this investigation turned out, innocent people were going to get hurt.

Ned walked them back to the dorm. George and Bess said good night and went upstairs. Nancy stayed with Ned a little longer.

He put an arm around her shoulders. "I'm sorry," he said softly, with his lips on her hair.

Nancy reached up and took his hand. "For what?"

"I so wanted us to have a fun, carefree time this weekend," he said. "Music and dancing. Lots of interesting people to meet and things to eat. It didn't exactly turn out that way."

"Don't be silly," Nancy said with a laugh. "We have had lots of music and dancing, and more to come. And the people I've met are certainly interesting . . . a little too much so! As for things to eat, well, I'll never forget that goulash."

"Are you sorry we roped you into investigating this case?" Ned asked.

"Not a bit," Nancy assured him. "It's a serious business, but besides that, it's fun. Not ha-ha fun, but exciting, involving . . . you know what I mean."

"I hoped you'd feel that way," Ned said. "I'd hate to think you held it against me."

"The only thing I want to hold against you is me,"
Nancy told him. She went on to prove that she meant
what she said.

Upstairs, Nancy unlocked the door to Dina's room
and opened it very quietly. A dim light shone in the far
corner.

"Nancy?" Dina said. "I'm still awake. I was waiting
for you."

"Sorry I'm back so late," Nancy said.

"It is I who must be sorry," Dina said, sitting up in
her bed. "I am so ashamed of myself. I have acted like
such a fool."

Nancy felt her shoulders tense up. Was Dina about
to admit that she stole the money?

"What do you mean?" Nancy asked cautiously.

Dina stood up and began to pace around the room.
"Once when I was little, my teacher said I was cheating
on a test. I screamed a terrible name at her. Then I tore
up my paper and ran from the room. I would not go
back to school. Every morning I screamed and cried
and made myself sick so my parents would keep me
home."

"How awful," Nancy said.

"Yes, it was," Dina said. "I do not excuse myself. I
gave my parents great concern. But at last the teacher
told the headmistress that I had not after all cheated.
The headmistress told my parents. When I returned to

school, I was moved to the class of a different teacher."

Nancy thought she saw where this was going. She began to relax.

"As I say," Dina continued, "I do not excuse myself. It is a failing. When I am accused of something I did not do, I become crazy. I strike out at everyone, friends and enemies alike. I say things I do not mean. I cannot help myself, it is my character. But afterward I am ashamed."

"You're talking about what happened tonight, with Vlad?" Nancy asked as she changed into pajamas.

"Of course," Dina said. "He and I have many issues between us. If he wrote that terrible e-mail, I will not forgive him. For him to say I was at the table before the money was taken . . . it was not kind, but it was true. I *was* there. I did not take the money. But was it unreasonable of him to wonder? I should have answered him, not attacked him."

"Nobody likes to be falsely accused," Nancy said. To herself she added a silent reminder. She should always be very sure of her ground before she accused someone of a crime.

"No, perhaps not," Dina said slowly. "But what do I do now? How do I show people that I am not a thief and not a crazy person, either?"

"When we find the real thief, your name will be cleared," Nancy pointed out. "As for the other thing, everybody knows you're under a lot of stress. If you show you're sorry and show more self-control, most of them will cut you some slack."

"I hope you are right," Dina said. She returned to her bed. "I do not care to be president of the IFC so much, but I do not want to lose the friends I have made here. If the only way to keep them is to stop being a candidate, I will do it in an instant!"

The next morning Nancy got up early, dressed, and went down to collect Bess and George. She reached the landing just as George came out of Joann's room.

"Hi, Nancy," George called cheerfully. She looked back through the doorway and said, "Take it easy, Joann. We'll see you later, after breakfast."

Nancy and George tapped on Penny's door. After a few moments, Penny opened it. Her pajamas and tousled hair showed she'd been asleep.

"I think Bess is still asleep," she whispered. She opened the door wider and stepped aside. Nancy and George followed her into the room.

"Well, she shouldn't be," George said in a normal tone of voice. "It's time to rise and shine. We've got a date."

"Hrmff grnnm." Bess's mumbled words were muffled by the pillow she had over her head.

A fiendish grin crossed George's face. She tiptoed over, took a corner of the pillow, and abruptly yanked it off. "Surprise!" she chirped. "It's morning!"

Bess let out a wail and reached blindly for the pillow. George dangled it just out of her reach. After a few moments Bess's expression changed from cross to resigned.

"All right, all right," she said, sitting up. "I'm awake. Sadist!"

George and Nancy waited while Bess dressed. Then the three friends started downstairs. Halfway to the main floor George said, "Oops, sorry. I have to go back. I didn't bring my sunglasses."

"No problem," Nancy said. "We'll go with you."

They climbed the stairs again. As they walked down the hall, George took out the key Joann had given her and said, "I won't be long. I know right where I left them."

She unlocked the door and pushed it open.

Joann was standing at her desk with her back to them. At the sound of the door, she spun around. Her face was contorted with fear. She spread her arms out as if to block the view of her desktop.

Too late. Nancy let out a gasp as she realized what she was looking at. Those thick stacks of green paper on the desk were money—*lots* of it.

12

Piles of Cash

"What do you want?" Joann cried. "Go away! Leave me alone!"

"We can't do that, Joann," Nancy said gently. "I'm afraid we need some explanation from you."

"I have nothing to say," Joann said, an edge of hysteria in her voice. "Nothing!"

"You'll have to talk to someone," George told her. "Wouldn't it be better us than the police?"

Joann's face went pale. She clutched the edge of the desk to keep from falling. "Police? Oh, no! That would be the end of everything for me!"

"Why don't you sit down?" Bess suggested. "And tell us about the money."

Joann looked behind her at the desk, as if she didn't

quite remember what was on it. Then she pulled out the desk chair and fell into it. "I don't know where to begin," she said faintly.

"We already know how badly you need money to stay at Emerson," Nancy said. "Did you take that envelope full of money at the dance last night?"

Joann stared at her. After a moment she said, "No, of course not. Is that what you think?"

"A bunch of money is missing," George pointed out. "And here you are with a bunch of unexplained money. You can't blame us for wondering."

"This money is mine," Joann said. Her voice strengthened. "My family sent it to me. Tomorrow I will use it to pay my college bill."

"Didn't you say there was a new law in your country against sending money abroad?" Nancy asked.

Joann looked away. "Yes," she agreed. "But my brother found a way. The money came with the shipment of wooden animals yesterday afternoon."

"Smuggled, you mean?" Bess asked.

Joann's cheeks turned pink. "I do not think it is against American law for my family to send me money," she said, raising her chin defiantly.

"Maybe not," Nancy said. "But here's the problem. We're trying to find out who took the IFC's money. If we don't succeed, very quickly, the police will have to be brought in. And unless we're really sure it has nothing to do with last night's theft, we'll have to tell them about finding you with all this cash."

"You mustn't," Joann declared. "If word got back to my country, my family would be put in terrible danger."

"We'll try to avoid that," Nancy assured her. "But what proof do we have that your story is true?"

Joann's shoulders slumped forward. "I don't know how to prove it. The money came just as I said. It was wrapped in newspapers, just like the wooden animals in the same carton. It came by air express. I can show you the carton and the express company receipt. Would that help?"

Nancy examined the receipt. The shipment had left Asia on Thursday. Joann had signed for it on Saturday. It wasn't proof, but it did fit with her account.

"Nancy?" George said. "Take a look at this." She was standing at the desk, studying the piles of cash. "You notice? There don't seem to be any of the new twenties and fifties, only the older version."

Nancy looked. George was right. She checked her own wallet. Two of the three twenties were the newer type with the huge portrait of Andrew Jackson.

"I see your point," Nancy said. "If this were the money from the dance last night, you'd expect some new bills."

"And not nearly so many fifties," George added. "Who pays to get into a college dance with a fifty-dollar bill?"

Bess joined them. She pointed to a stack of bills near the bottom of the pile. "What's that paper band?" she wondered.

Joann looked puzzled. "That is nothing odd," she said. "When the bank counts money, it always puts such a band on it."

"May we see?" Nancy asked.

Joann pulled out the bills. They appeared to be all old-style twenties. The brown paper band was stamped with the name of a bank in the capital of Joann's country.

"I don't see how that could have come from the dance," George said. "I'm satisfied."

"So am I," Bess said. "I'm glad I noticed it."

Nancy knew the banded bills supported Joann's story but didn't actually prove it. Still, it was as close as they were likely to come at this point.

"We'd better go," Nancy said. "We may have more questions later. And if I were you, I'd save the carton and all the packing material. If the police take over the case, they'll want to examine them."

"Of course," Joann said, looking scared again at the mention of the police. "I'll be careful."

Nancy, George, and Bess hurried to the pancake restaurant, where they were to meet Ned, Cyril, and J. P.

"Bad news," Ned said, waiting just outside the entrance. "There's a half hour wait for a table. I put our names down, but I think we'd better go somewhere that'll take us right away. We can't be late for the steering committee meeting."

"I noticed a neat-looking French bakery on the way here," Bess said. "Why not just get pastries and coffee and sit on the grass somewhere? If we still need a real meal, we can eat after the meeting."

The others liked the idea. A few minutes later they were enjoying a picnic breakfast in a college garden. Between bites, Nancy told the guys about Joann and the cash. "We'd better keep it to ourselves," she concluded. "If the story got around, it really might cause problems for her family."

"Too right," Cyril said. "But I hope Joann doesn't overlook Scrooge's Law."

Bess eyed him. "Is that the one that goes, If you have a fifty/fifty chance, you lose?"

Cyril grinned at her. "Close, luv. Actually the version I know is, If there's anything you don't want people to find out, they will."

Nancy recalled Cyril's words later, when the IFC steering committee assembled in a meeting room at the student center.

"I hate to tell you," Penny said. "I got a call half an hour ago from a guy who's a reporter on the *Emersonian*. He wanted to check out a rumor he'd heard. Was it true that somebody made off with all the proceeds of the Worldbeat Festival?"

Cyril groaned and put his head in his hands.

"I put him off," Penny continued. "But he's not going to stop digging. If we want our point of view to be heard, we'll have to talk to him."

"How long do we have?" Akai asked.

"They go to press around eleven at night," J. P. said. "But breaking stories can be posted on the paper's Web site as they come in."

"Penny?" Cyril asked. "Can you get your friend to hold off until after the concert this afternoon?"

"I can try," Penny said, but did not sound very confident.

Cyril turned to Nancy. "Any chance you'll have an answer by then?"

"We can try," Nancy replied. Her tone, like her words, echoed Penny's.

"This reporter," Vlad said. "What right does he have to pry into our private affairs?"

Dina gave a snort of disgust. "In this country," she said, "the people have a right to know what is happening. It is not like some countries, where they are expected to act like sheep."

Cyril sighed. "Can we at least make a feeble effort to stay on-topic?" he asked. "Completely apart from the emergency over the theft last night, we have to make ready for this afternoon's concert."

"We'd better not lose the money from that, too," a girl with short brown hair said. "Who's taking care of it today?"

Penny glared at her. "Listen, Consuelo. It wasn't Lance's fault the money disappeared, if that's what you're implying."

"I'm not implying anything," Consuelo replied. "But he *was* in charge of it. Where is he, anyway?"

"He had a lot of stuff to do in connection with the bike trip," Penny explained. "He said he'd try to get here before we finish."

"Good," Cyril said. He looked down at his notes. "Dina? How about a treasurer's report? What's the financial picture of the club at this point?"

"I'm sorry," Dina said. "I've had no time to prepare. I will have everything ready for our next meeting."

"Does this committee have no right to know?" Vlad asked in an ironic tone. "Are we expected to act like sheep? Or perhaps like the blind?"

"What do you mean?" Dina demanded hotly.

"Questions have been asked about the club's finances," Vlad retorted. "Is it not strange that you brought nothing—no records, no balance sheets—to this meeting? Why is that? Are you afraid of what we might see if we looked at them?"

"I am afraid of nothing you may say or do!" Dina declared. "Cyril, I insist that the steering committee examine the club's books—immediately!"

"I don't think—" Cyril began.

"I mean it," Dina said. She jumped to her feet. "Now! Right away!"

Nancy could almost read Cyril's mind. Would it take less time and energy to give in to Dina's demand, or to go on arguing about it?

"Very well," he said.

Five minutes later the members of the IFC steering committee, plus Nancy, Bess, and George, trooped into Dina's room. They crowded around her desk and watched while she turned on her computer.

"You will see now," she said, turning around to face them. "There is nothing—"

From the computer speakers came a loud, rude noise.

Nancy stared.

Instead of the usual opening screen, the monitor showed a cartoon face with its tongue stuck out. Under it, in big splashy letters, was the message:

HA! HA! YOU'RE HOSED, SUCKER!

13

Virus Attack!

Dina read the mocking message on her computer screen. The blood drained from her face. "What—!" she gasped. "I don't understand."

She grabbed the mouse. She tried to open one file, then another and another. Each time she did, a box with a big exclamation point came on the screen.

> DISK ERROR: THE FILE 'FINREC.IFC' HAS BECOME CORRUPTED.
>
> IT CANNOT BE OPENED BY THIS PROGRAM. MESSAGE -32H

"Why is this happening?" Dina wailed. "It is never like this!"

Joann pushed to the front of the crowd. "I think your computer has been infected by a virus," she said. "Let me see if I can do anything."

"I'm going to call Lance," Penny announced. "I bet he can help." She stepped away and pulled out a cell phone.

Nancy peered over Joann's shoulder as she typed a series of commands. After a few moments she straightened up and said, "It looks to me as if the disk directory has been damaged."

"This is a disaster," Dina said. "What do I do? My notes, my research papers, my letters home. . . ."

"*And* all the IFC's financial records," Vlad said in an undertone.

Cyril and J. P. glared at him. Dina didn't hear or at least didn't respond.

"It could be a lot worse," Joann told Dina. "If I'm right, a specialist can recover almost all your data. It takes time, though, and it is not cheap."

Nancy stepped forward. "Joann, do you have any idea how this could have happened? Some problem with the computer hardware?"

Joann shook her head. "I do not think so. A faulty hard disk does not put an insulting message on the screen. As I said, the most likely cause is a virus. That is a destructive program that infects the computer from outside and damages the files and programs."

"Infects it how?" Bess asked.

Joann frowned. "Most often, the virus is concealed

in an e-mail attachment. When you open the attachment, the program installs itself on your machine and goes to work."

"Dina?" Nancy said. Dina didn't look up. Nancy touched her shoulder and repeated, "Dina? Did you get any e-mail messages with attachments lately?"

Dina blinked a couple of times, then said, "Only one, yesterday. But it was a mistake. When I looked at the attachment, it was blank."

Nancy glanced over at Joann. She nodded. That was probably how the virus arrived.

"Do you remember who sent it?" Nancy asked Dina.

Her forehead wrinkled. "Who? Of course. It was Vlad. I could not understand why he would send me a joke. It was not even very funny."

"I?" Vlad exclaimed. "I would never send jokes by e-mail. They are the pest of the century. When I see one in my box, I always delete it unread."

"The point isn't the joke," George told him. "It looks as if the virus came along with it."

Nancy saw Vlad's face change. It seemed he had just realized what he was being accused of.

"To deliberately destroy someone's records?" he said. "Sheer vandalism! That would be as bad as burning their books. No, no. It is not possible you think I would do such a thing. Dina . . . ?"

Dina looked at him. She seemed torn. "No, I don't believe—" she began. "But politics makes people do terrible things for what seem like good reasons. I don't know. I don't know."

The door banged open. Lance stood there, out of breath. His madras plaid shirt had been buttoned crooked and was only partly tucked in.

"The virus hit me, too!" he announced. "All my files, trashed!"

"Lucky you keep backup copies of everything," Cyril observed. "You *did* tell me that's what you do, didn't you?"

"Er . . . no," Lance said, suddenly sheepish. "What I told you was how important it is to keep backups. The fact is, I've been so busy the last few weeks that I didn't get around to it."

"Oh, Lance," Penny said. "You mean, all the records for the bike trip this summer?"

"Gone-zo," Lance said. "I guess I can reconstruct them from the forms people filled out, but it'll be a major pain."

"You'd better get right on it," Penny said. "Don't you have to give the travel agency a big payment next week?"

"Never mind that," Lance said brusquely. "I'll take care of it."

"How do you suppose the virus got to your computer?" Ned asked. "You didn't get an e-mail from Vlad yesterday, did you?"

"I resent that!" Vlad proclaimed.

Lance looked puzzled. "Vlad? No, why?"

"Any e-mail with an attachment that you opened?" Nancy asked.

"No, only. . . ." Lance looked at Dina. "I meant to ask you. What was so urgent about that message yesterday? When I tried to open the file you attached to it, it was blank."

Dina's face was blank, too. "I sent you no message yesterday," she said.

"Your name was on it," Lance said.

"I didn't send anyone anything yesterday," Dina insisted. "Not you, not anyone!"

"That's the way some viruses work," Nancy explained. "Once it's on your computer, it hunts up your e-mail address book and sends itself to some or all the names it finds. Dina, Lance—you'd better alert everyone you know. They shouldn't open any e-mail attachments that claim they're from you."

"Good point," Lance said. "That didn't occur to me."

"Please excuse me," Joann said shyly. "The bazaar will open soon. I must get my booth ready."

"And we'd better get some lunch before we have to set up for the concert," Cyril pointed out. "Do I hear a motion to adjourn?"

Everyone followed him out. Nancy paused to get a scarf from her knapsack. As she left the room, she glanced back. Dina was still sitting at her desk. She was hunched over her corrupted computer with her face buried in her hands.

Outside, Nancy rejoined the little clump of IFC members, just as Lance said, "Penny and I had better run. We have a brunch reservation at the Old Drovers Inn. I still have to dress."

Penny glanced down at her faded jeans and running shoes. "Me, too," she said with a grin.

"You'll be back in time for the concert, won't you?" Cyril asked in a worried voice.

"No problem," Lance assured him. "But please, don't ask me to collect admissions. I don't want the responsibility. Maybe lightning doesn't strike twice, but the thieves might."

After Lance and Penny had left, J. P. remarked, "Brunch at the Old Drovers? Sounds nice."

"Too right it does," Cyril said. "I mean to try it myself one day . . . after I win the lottery."

"Meanwhile," Ned said with a glance at Nancy, "how about the salad bar at Commons? We can grab a couple of tables on the terrace."

"Sounds good," Nancy said.

After lunch Cyril, Ned, and J. P. went to check out the preparations for the concert. Nancy, Bess, and George promised to meet them at the quad later. They left campus and asked directions to the grocery store where somebody had bought salt and artificial sweetener on Friday.

The place turned out to be a busy convenience store

and gas station. The woman behind the counter listened to their question in between ringing up other customers. She turned and shouted toward the rear of the store, "Jerry? C'mere a minute?"

A guy of about twenty came out of a back room and ambled over to them. He had a rose tattooed on his wrist and a pack of cigarettes tucked into the pocket of his T-shirt.

"Yeah?" he said. "What is it?"

Nancy showed him the register receipt. "Do you happen to remember who bought this?" she asked. "It was on Friday, the day before yesterday, in the middle of the afternoon."

Jerry stared at her. "You're kidding, right?" he said. "Sister, do you have any idea how many people we get in here every hour?"

Nancy felt a spurt of irritation at being called *Sister* by this guy. She pushed it back and said, "Just two items, salt and sweetener. That's a little odd. Maybe it rings a bell?"

"Half our customers buy weird stuff," Jerry told her. "That's what keeps us in business."

Without another word he turned and walked away. Nancy exchanged glances with Bess and George. Bess looked indignant. George rolled her eyes.

"Thanks," Nancy muttered to the woman at the register as they left. Under her breath, she added, "For a big fat nothing."

The three girls walked back to campus. They found

the quad transformed. The rear section had been turned into a concert arena. The booths of the bazaar flanked the path back to the gate. They reminded Nancy of the sideshows on the way in to an old-fashioned circus big top.

"I say we prowl around and watch for trouble," George suggested.

"I want to talk to the exhibitors," Bess said. "Maybe one of them's noticed something helpful."

Nancy smiled to herself. Bess could never pass up a chance to do some serious shopping.

"I'll be backstage," Nancy said. "I still can't believe no one saw whoever untied the tent ropes yesterday."

A wooden sawhorse blocked the entrance to the performing area. When Nancy started to slide by it, a campus security officer hurried over and blocked her way. "Sorry, you'll have to wait outside," he said. "Only those with cards are allowed in."

Cyril was twenty feet away, talking to a couple of stagehands. He noticed Nancy and called, "She's okay, Skip. She's part of the crew. Let her by."

Skip stepped aside.

The whole back part of the quad was now filled with hundreds of folding chairs. The stage had been made at least twenty feet wider and ten deeper than the day before. Imposing speaker towers loomed on each side of it. Behind the stage a second green-and-yellow tent had joined the one Nancy remembered so well.

Nancy started down the center aisle toward the stage. She noticed that soundboards and light boards had been installed on a platform about eight feet up, in the middle of the rows of seats. A ladder at the back led up to the platform, and cloth panels tied to the railings screened it from view.

As Nancy walked by, one of the cloth panels fluttered in the breeze. She was two steps farther along when she realized that there wasn't any breeze. She turned and stared. The panel was still now. Had she imagined the motion? Maybe, but she didn't think so. She had better check.

She walked back and started up the ladder. When her head was level with the floor of the platform, she paused to study the space. Directly across from her were the light board and the soundboard. Thick bunches of cables snaked down from each. Two stacks of black fiberboard equipment cases hid the ends of the platform from her.

She scrambled up the remaining rungs and stepped cautiously over to peer behind the nearest stack of cases. There was nothing there but a crumpled, empty corn chip bag.

Behind her a shoe scraped on the plywood floor. Nancy started to turn. Suddenly a paper bag was pulled down over her head. Two strong hands closed around her upper arms. She took a deep breath and prepared to twist free. Before she could, however, she was hurled to the left.

The bag blinded her, but she knew what was in that direction: the gap in the railing where the ladder was attached. And beyond that, nothing . . . only a shattering fall onto rows of metal chairs.

14

A Shocking Plot

Off balance, Nancy staggered sideways. She flung her arms wide. Her fingers groped for anything she could grasp to save herself. As she fell to her knees, her right hand brushed against a bare arm. She tried to grab it, but another shove pushed her away. She heard the clatter of shoes on the steel ladder. Her attacker was escaping!

Nancy's hip struck the plywood floor. A sharp edge dug into her painfully, but she had no time to pay attention to that because from the waist up, there was nothing under her. She was falling off the platform.

Frantically, she twisted on to her stomach. If she was falling through the gap, the rungs of the ladder must be right below her. She reached down as far as she could.

Her left forearm banged against something cold and hard. Instantly she pulled her arms up and locked her fingers around the steel rung. Moments later she felt her legs slide off the platform. She jackknifed at the waist and did a forward somersault in midair. Could her arms and hands take the sudden strain?

Nancy's back slammed into the lower part of the ladder. Her arms felt as if they were pulling loose from her shoulder sockets. She gasped in pain and tried to catch her breath.

"Nancy! Hold on!" Ned shouted. "Hold on!"

She held on. At the same time she felt around with her feet. Was there anything to stand on, any way to take some of the burden off her aching shoulders?

Just as her heel banged into one of the lower rungs of the ladder, she felt familiar hands clasp her around the waist. "Okay!" Ned said. "I've got you. You can let go."

Her fingers did not want to release their grip on the ladder. Finally Ned lowered her to the ground. She tore the paper bag off her head. The fresh air tasted very sweet.

Half a dozen people crowded around her. "What happened?" they demanded, all talking at once. "Did someone attack you? Who was it?"

Nancy cleared her throat. It felt very dry. "I don't

know," she said. "Somebody was hiding up on the platform. When I went to check it out, he tried to push me off."

" 'Tried'?" Ned repeated grimly. "He *did* push you off! It's a miracle you weren't badly hurt."

Nancy managed a weak smile. "I owe it all to my gymnastics teacher back in fifth grade," she joked. "I don't know what the guy was up to, messing with the light and sound boards, but somebody should check them out."

"I'll do it," one of the tech crew volunteered. He swung up the ladder.

"We need to talk," Nancy told Ned in a low voice. He followed her off to one side. The other onlookers took the hint and went about their business.

"I think our bad guy just made a major boo-boo," Nancy continued.

"You better believe it," Ned replied. "When I catch up with him, he is ancient history!"

"That's not what I mean," Nancy said. "When I came in just now, a guard stopped me. He said I needed a card. Cyril had to tell him to let me in."

"Right," Ned said. He reached into his shirt and fished up an ID card on a metal chain. In large print it read, Worldbeat Weekend—Official. "We should have made these up for you three. I guess no one thought of it."

"Water under the bridge," Nancy said. "My point is,

whoever was up on the platform either has one of those cards or was vouched for by someone who does. Can you get us a list of cardholders, right away?"

"I'll ask Cyril," Ned promised. "I'll get cards for you and George and Bess, too."

"Hey," a voice called from above them. The techie was at the railing of the platform. He looked furious. "I found out what that lowlife was doing up here. He stripped the insulation off some of the light cables and taped them to the metal scaffold."

"What would that do?" Nancy asked, even though she was pretty sure she knew the answer.

The guy gestured toward the lights over the stage. "The minute we powered up the spots, we'd have blown every circuit breaker between here and the Canadian border. And I wouldn't want to be leaning against the scaffolding when it happened. _Z–z–z–zap!_ Just like one of those bug lamps."

"Can you fix the damage in time for the concert?" Ned asked.

"No problemo," the technician replied. "I'll get right on it."

Bess and George came rushing up. "Nancy!" Bess cried. "We just heard!"

"Are you okay?" George asked with concern.

"I'm fine," Nancy assured them. "But we have work to do. Our saboteur is getting desperate. It's just a matter of time before somebody gets hurt."

"I'll talk to Cyril, right away," Ned offered. "We'll have to tighten our security even more."

"What should we do?" George asked as Ned left.

Nancy turned one of the folding chairs and sat down. The moment the weight was off her legs, she realized how much her near fall had exhausted her. She waved her friends into chairs facing her.

"We can't be security guards," she said. "We have to be detectives. What is this case about?"

"Winning the IFC election by making the other guy look bad?" Bess suggested.

"That's what I thought, too, at first," Nancy said. "But how does spoiling someone's goulash do that? Or sending out a computer virus? Or blowing the lights at the big concert?"

"How about wrecking the Worldbeat Weekend?" George said.

Nancy nodded. "That's pretty clear," she said. "But why? Just plain meanness? Somebody is going to a lot of trouble and taking a lot of risks. He has to have a pretty strong motive."

"I'll buy that," George said. "But what?"

"Revenge," Bess said. "Or rivalry. Some other campus club wants to destroy the IFC."

"If we stand back and look at everything that's happened," Nancy said, "one event stands out, because it's so different from the others. The e-mails and phone calls and viruses, the salt in the stew, even monkeying with the light cables—they're all some form of dirty trick. What if their purpose is to distract us from the one real, solid crime?"

"Stealing the money!" George exclaimed.

Bess frowned. "You mean, whoever took the money didn't do it to wreck the festival? He wrecked the festival to confuse everyone about the theft?"

"That's what I think," Nancy replied. "The thread that links all this is that somebody has an urgent and terribly important need for money."

"Hold on," George said. She looked troubled. "I thought we decided Joann was telling the truth about where she got that money."

"Anyway," Bess added, "she couldn't have pushed you off the platform just now. I'd been talking to her at her booth for five or ten minutes when I heard about your fall."

"What about Dina?" George asked. "She *is* the club treasurer. Maybe that e-mail was right. If she embezzled club money to send to some extremist group in her country, she might have stolen last night's proceeds to use to cover her tracks."

"Hey, yeah," Bess said excitedly. "And then she deliberately destroyed her computer records so no one would find out."

"The files aren't destroyed, just harder to get to," Nancy pointed out. "And I don't think she faked that threatening phone call the other night. But mainly, I do not believe she would have ruined her goulash. I saw how much that upset her."

"So who's your candidate?" Bess asked.

"Motive, means, and opportunity," Nancy said. "Those are the three things my dad always tells me to look for when I'm investigating a crime. What about the theft? We can come back to motive, and we know the means—that decoy envelope. But who had an opportunity to carry out the substitution?"

"Joann again," George said.

"Dina," Bess said. "Plus whoever staged the fight between those two guys."

"Two guys who were seen by only one person," Nancy pointed out. "And that person was alone with the real envelope for longer than anyone else."

George stared at her. "You mean Lance? But he didn't have a chance to take the money. He was at the gym the whole time. Why do you suspect him?"

"Ned told me he's here on a scholarship," Nancy replied. "But Penny is convinced he's well off. Where is he getting the money to take her to all these fancy restaurants?"

"His clothes cost a lot, too," Bess observed.

Nancy snapped her fingers. "Bess, that's it!" she exclaimed. "I *knew* there was some detail I was overlooking. Listen—when Lance showed up to start collecting money last night, he was wearing a coat and tie. But when he came to tell everyone the money was gone, he was in a maroon polo shirt. When did he change?"

"Maybe he had the shirt with him," George suggested hesitantly.

"Maybe," Nancy replied. "But then what did he do with his other shirt and his sport coat? I think he took the money back to his room and changed while he was there."

"We'd better find him," George said. "He deserves a chance to tell his side of the story."

They stood up. Just then a crowd of eager students started flowing through the gate. Nancy spotted Ned and Cyril near the gate and waved urgently. The two guys hurried over.

"Have you seen Lance?" she asked them.

"I did a moment ago," Cyril told her. "He's outside the gate, making a call."

"I'll be right back," Nancy said. She worked her way against the flow of the crowd. At the gate she waited for a gap and pushed through.

Lance was just a few feet away, his back to her. He had a cell phone pressed to his ear. As Nancy drew closer, she heard him say, "It's just for a week or two, Aunt Ellie. Just until the estate is settled. You know I'll pay you back. It's really important."

A light breeze brought Nancy a whiff of Lance's aftershave lotion. She recognized it. She had smelled it just a few minutes before, on the person who had tried to push her off the platform.

Nancy felt a wave of anger break over her. She reached out and grabbed Lance roughly by the collar.

Startled, he whirled to face her. When he saw her expression, he realized that she had unmasked him. He drew back his arm and hurled his cell phone at her head.

15

Facing the Music

A split second before Lance threw the cell phone at her, Nancy ducked. The phone whizzed past her, grazing her earlobe, and sailed into the booth behind her. It crashed onto a table stacked with jars of exotic spices.

"Hey!" the spice seller yelled. "What the—!"

Lance bulled his way through the waiting crowd. At the gate he waved his card. The security man stepped aside and let him through.

Nancy tried to follow Lance. The crowd blocked her way. "Please," she begged. "Let me through! It's important!"

They ignored her. Lance had just shoved past them. They were not going to let another line-jumper get by, too.

Finally Nancy managed to wriggle and worm her way to the gate. The security man stopped her. "Sorry, ticketholders only," he said.

"You let me in before," Nancy reminded him. "I'm staff. Cyril vouched for me. Remember?"

The man shook his head. "Sorry, miss. Now, will you please move out of the way? These people want to go in."

"Yeah, move it!" somebody shouted from behind her.

It felt as if a riot were about to break out, with her as the target. Nancy looked around the area inside. Was there anybody who knew her? Just when she was about to give up, she spotted Akai. He was twenty feet away, talking to a girl wearing a colorful African tribal robe and headdress.

Nancy called his name. It took him a few moments to locate her. He hurried over and asked the guard to let her in. Even after he showed his own staff card, the guard balked. Finally Akai moved the barrier aside and motioned Nancy in. The security man did not like it, but there was nothing he could do.

By now, of course, Lance had managed to lose himself in the crowd. Nancy walked quickly to the front of the seating area, then started up the center aisle more slowly, scanning the faces on either side. George, Bess, and Ned soon noticed her and hurried to join her.

"Ned," Nancy said after she had explained about Lance, "will you cover the entrance? We'll search the crowd."

"Check," Ned said.

"George, take the left side," Nancy continued. "And Bess, the right. I'll stay in the middle. If you see any of our friends, get them in on it, too."

The three girls fanned out. Nancy continued walking slowly up the center aisle. By now there were hundreds of students waiting for the music to begin. Some had already taken their seats, but most were standing in clumps, talking. Lance could be hidden in the middle of any of them. He could also be anywhere backstage.

As Nancy neared the scaffold that held the sound and light boards, she saw Penny coming toward her. She tensed up. Penny was Lance's girlfriend. Was she also his accomplice?

"Hi, Nancy," Penny said. "Listen, is anything wrong with Lance?"

"Why?" Nancy asked cautiously.

"Well . . ." Penny hesitated, then said, "When I saw him just now, he acted very weird. He pretended not to see me. Why would he do that?"

"Where was this?" Nancy asked. She tried not to spook Penny by sounding too eager.

Penny waved toward the far corner of the rows of chairs. "Over there," she said. "He was sitting with a bunch of people I didn't know. He had his head down like he was reading. But I didn't see anything on his lap. And I'm sure he saw me. What's going on?"

Penny sounded sincerely puzzled. Still, Nancy won-

141

dered if this was a ploy on Lance's part to throw her off his track. She had to take that risk.

"I'll go talk to him," Nancy told Penny, and walked quickly in the direction Penny had indicated.

More of the crowd was seated now. The rows of faces blurred into featureless ovals, all aimed toward the stage. As Nancy neared the back of the arena, however, she spotted one squarish head that was bent over, showing only neatly trimmed blond hair.

"Hey, Lance, over here," Nancy called.

Startled, Lance raised his head. When he saw Nancy, his eyes widened in alarm. He jumped to his feet and started edging past his neighbors toward the far aisle. The angry cries showed that he was stepping on quite a few toes.

Nancy stayed where she was. George had seen what was happening and was waiting for Lance at the other end of the row. And if that wasn't enough, J. P. was hurrying up the aisle to join George.

Bess came running over. "We caught him!" she exulted.

"Looks that way," Nancy agreed as George and J. P. walked Lance toward the exit.

From the stage came a loud chord. The audience cheered as a folk-rock group from Montreal charged full-tilt into a fast tune. It sounded half Irish and half French. Both halves rocked.

* * *

After turning Lance over to the local police, Nancy and her friends returned for the rest of the concert. Cyril had saved them seats down front. Nancy loved hearing the different groups from around the world. It was a real education. Cuban, Dominican, and Haitian musicians, from within a hundred miles of each other, had distinctive sounds. Yet all of them had so much in common with the harmonies and rhythms of the West Africans and Latin Americans. Maybe there really *was* a Worldbeat!

Nancy's favorite moment came during the Rai Rebels' set. Cheb Rachid began a haunting tune backed by a techno mix. In the middle he came to the front of the stage. Kneeling by the edge, he sang the rest of the song looking straight into Bess's eyes. The words were in Arabic, but his gaze spoke a universal language. Bess practically melted into her seat.

After the concert Nancy and her friends joined the members of the IFC steering committee at the student center. Cyril was the last to arrive. He came in wearing an odd smile and shaking his head.

"I was just on the phone to the police station," he said.

"What's happened?" Joann asked. "Did Lance confess?"

"Some hope!" Cyril said. "He's not talking. His lawyer claims the whole thing is an honest mistake. Lance took the money to his room to protect it. Then he spread the tale that it had been stolen as a way of bluffing any thieves who might be after it."

Nancy let out a snort of disbelief. "What about pushing me off the platform this afternoon?" she asked. "Was that an honest mistake?"

Cyril gave her a sympathetic look. "Well, luv, he's not charged with that, is he now? And it's not as if you got a look at him."

"You mean, he's going to get away with it?" George demanded indignantly.

"I didn't say that," Cyril replied. "Speaking for myself, I doubt it. The courts aren't daft. But it is quite a cute tale, isn't it?"

"But what's the real story?" Dina asked. "Was it Lance the whole time? What was he after?"

Cyril gave Nancy a nod.

Nancy cleared her throat. "Some of this is guesswork," she admitted. "But it fits the facts as we know them. This case started a couple of months ago, when Lance inherited a fair amount of money from an uncle."

"Lucky Lance," J. P. murmured.

"Yes and no," George told him. "He has expensive tastes. Now he could indulge them. So he did. Clothes, gourmet meals . . ."

"Sounds good to me," Vlad said. "What is the problem?"

"What's called probate," Nancy replied. "It can take weeks or even months before you actually collect money you've inherited. And Lance didn't want to wait. He started spending money he didn't have."

"You mean, credit cards?" Joann asked.

"Worse," Bess said. "The deposits people gave him for the bicycle trip this summer. Instead of putting them in a bank account, he spent them."

"I don't think he thought of it as stealing," Nancy added. "He meant to replace what he'd spent as soon as he got his uncle's money. But that was taking longer and longer. And he had to pay a big sum to the travel agency next week."

"That's the reason he decided to make off with the proceeds from the picnic and the dance," George said. "He could use that money to make the payment on the bike trip, then pretend to discover it once he had his inheritance."

"Or not," Ned said. "If you ask me, we would never have seen that money again."

After a short silence Dina said, "I am still confused. What was the reason for the e-mail and the telephone calls and the computer bug and the rest?"

"What magicians call misdirection," Nancy explained. "If the disappearance of the money had been the only incident, Lance would have been the obvious suspect. The commotion over the IFC election was ideal for him. If he could get you and Vlad at each other's throats, everybody would assume that the theft, like all the other incidents, was part of your battle."

"So Lance did it all?" Joann asked.

"We think so," Nancy said. "He probably doctored

the two dishes before they were even brought to the gym. As for the virus that hit Dina's computer, that should have tipped us off. Lance was one of the few real computer experts in the club. He threw us off the track by infecting his own files as well . . . or pretending to."

"That also gave him a way to get rid of the bike trip records, which might have incriminated him," George pointed out.

"You know," Cyril said slowly, "what happened to Lance is a bit like what happens when countries fall afoul of each other. He simply kept digging himself deeper into a hole. By the end he was so far gone that he was ready to push Nancy off that platform."

Vlad stood up. "I am ashamed," he announced. "If I had not been so ready to believe the worst of Dina, Lance could not have carried out this vile scheme. Dina, I apologize. I will withdraw my name from the presidency race and urge everyone to vote for you."

"No, no," Dina said. "It is I who must apologize. I let myself be imprisoned by outworn ideas. I am not fit to lead the IFC. I intend to support you for president."

Vlad scowled. "I cannot allow such a gesture," he declared. "You must be president!"

"No, you!" Dina retorted angrily.

Nancy looked over at George and Bess. All three started to laugh. Dina and Vlad glared at them. Then, as the others in the room joined in, they relaxed and managed to smile.

"Perhaps a co-presidency," Vlad suggested.

"Excellent proposal," Dina replied. "It must be given serious consideration. Are you free after supper?"

Nancy turned to Ned and winked. "You know," she murmured, "there may be some hope for international friendship after all!"

**Do your younger brothers and sisters
want to read books like yours?**

**Let them know there
are books just for *them!***

They can join Nancy Drew and her best
friends as they collect clues and solve
mysteries in

THE

NANCY DREW

NOTEBOOKS®

Starting with
#1 The Slumber Party Secret
#2 The Lost Locket
#3 The Secret Santa
#4 Bad Day for Ballet

AND

**Meet up with suspense and mystery
in The Hardy Boys are: The Clues Brothers™**

Starting with
#1 The Gross Ghost Mystery
#2 The Karate Clue
#3 First Day, Worst Day
#4 Jump Shot Detectives

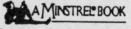 A MINSTREL BOOK

Published by Pocket Books

2324

American S·I·S·T·E·R·S

Join different sets of sisters
as they embark on the varied,
sometimes dangerous,
always exciting journeys
across America's landscape!

West Along the Wagon Road, 1852

≈

A *Titanic* Journey Across the Sea, 1912

≈

Voyage to a Free Land, 1630

≈

Adventure on the Wilderness Road, 1775

≈

Crossing the Colorado Rockies, 1864

≈

Down the Rio Grande, 1829

by Laurie Lawlor

A MINSTREL® BOOK

Published by Pocket Books

2200-02